BABY GIRL III

SCOTT

Author's Note

If you have to question your love - if you don't know for certain that it is *truly* love - stop.

Stop living a life of misery and being filled with wonder.

Look.

That person is out there.

Waiting.

And when you find them, you'll know.

You won't wonder.

You'll know.

Because you'll have it.

Love that just is.

Dedication

This book is dedicated to all the men and women that have found true love – and those that haven't.

Again, a special thanks to Sis, A-Train, and The Bone for being patient.

A special thanks to the men and women who ride. Live for it, because it lives within us.

Lastly…

Bama, you owe me a drink. Make it water.

And make it a double.

This book is a work of fiction. Names, characters, places, and incidents are the product of the author's imagination or are used fictitiously. Any resemblances to actual events, locales, or persons living or dead, are coincidental.

Copyright © 2013 by Scott Hildreth

All rights reserved. In accordance with the U.S. Copyright Act of 1976, the scanning, uploading, and electronic sharing of any part of this book without the permission of the author or publisher constitute unlawful piracy and theft of the author's intellectual property. If you would like to use the material from the book (other than for review purposes), prior written permission must be obtained by contacting the author at designconceptswichita@gmail.com. Thank you for your support of the author's rights.

Chapter One

*E*RIK. "Do you like it?" I asked as she rocked back and forth on the passenger portion of the seat.

"It's *really* comfortable. This is so soft," she said as she pressed down on the front of the seat with the palms of her hands.

"You don't like that red one?" she asked, pointing to a burgundy colored similar model across the sales floor.

"No. Bikes should only come in one color. *Black*," I responded, smiling.

"Mr. uhmm...?" the salesman stammered as he walked in front of the bike, holding a portfolio.

"Erik," I responded.

"Mr. Erik, we can go twenty-two thousand even. That's the best we can do," he said, pointing to the portfolio.

"Erik, not Mr. Erik. My name is Erik. And what did I tell you? I said twenty grand. Or we'd walk. I'm a man of principle. I'll walk over fifty bucks. It's a 2013 model. The riding season is over, and the 2014 models are out. I will give twenty, and we'll ride that black mother-fucker off the floor," I said as I pointed to the door.

Kelli grabbed ahold of the handlebars, and scooted forward on the seat. Sitting on the bike as if riding it, she was a different degree of beautiful. In the future, she will have to get a license to ride, and a bike of her own.

"It makes you feel powerful when you have ahold of the handlebars," she said as she turned to face me.

"Ma'am, be careful. The bike can tip over. Maybe you should just get off of it," the salesman said as he turned toward Kelli.

"Maybe you should watch your tone of voice with her," I said as I took a step in his direction.

SCOTT

"It's ok," Kelli said as she started to raise her leg over the seat.

"Don't you dare get off that bike," I said in a stern tone.

She nestled into the seat and smiled.

"Sir, the bike can tip over, she should..."

My jaw tightened.

"I'm going to give you one more chance to shut the fuck up," I whispered in his direction.

The salesman froze.

"How's that go, baby girl?" I raised one eyebrow and looked at Kelli.

"Never miss a good opportunity to keep your fucking mouth shut," she laughed, nodding her head sharply as she finished saying it.

He looked at her and closed the portfolio. He turned and looked at me. He looked around the sales floor, as if to see if someone was willing to assist him. There wasn't another sales associate within eyeshot.

"Put the twelve inch apes on it, and the true duals. We'll give the twenty-two," I said toward the salesman.

"Uhhmm...." He opened the portfolio and flipped through the pages.

"That's. That's about," he flipped through the pages, "that's two grand in extras."

"Maybe *here* it is. Not in the real world. Twenty-two with the accessories, our final offer," I said.

"We can't do that," he said.

"You *can*. You just won't. Topeka will. Kansas City will. Tulsa will. It's disappointing. I try to spend money locally. This place...it's any wonder you stay in business," I shook my head.

"We have overhead we have to pay," he said as he stuffed the portfolio under his armpit.

"Everyone does. Get down, baby girl," I said as I pointed toward Kelli.

She tried not to look disappointed as she stepped over the seat. She stood beside the bike and turned toward it, admiring it.

"Baby girl?" I said as she straightened the wrinkles from her jeans.

"Sir?" she responded, turning my direction.

"Who? Who owns you baby girl?" I asked softly, holding my arms out at my sides, palms turned upward.

"You. You sir," she responded, smiling. She began to walk toward me.

Such simple words. She can't come close to hiding the satisfaction that she feels when I remind her.

She put her arms around me and squeezed, her face buried in my shirt. She took a deep breath. "I like smelling you," she said as she looked up.

"I like being smelled by you," I said as I kissed her lips lightly.

"So?" the salesman asked in our direction.

"I already told you what we would do," I responded.

"We just can't…"

"We've been through this. You have *overhead*. I get it," I said.

"If financing is an issue, Harley-Davidson has great financing," he smiled and raised his eyebrows.

I shook my head and turned toward the door.

"Come on, baby. Let's go," I said as I took a step toward the door.

"I like baggers," Kelli said as we walked toward the door.

"I thought it was really nice too. We'll get one, just not here," I said as we walked toward the door.

She nodded her head a few times and grabbed my left arm.

"Doc Ead!" a familiar voice shouted as we approached the door.

King stepped through the door, smiling. He held his hand out.

"How you doing, King?" I said as I shook his hand.

"Fine, Doc. Just fine," he said as he patted me on the shoulder with his left hand.

"You must be *Sis*," he said as he turned toward Kelli.

Kelli looked up into my eyes. I winked. She looked at King and nodded.

"I heard Doc had a beautiful woman, but I had no idea," he held his hand out toward Kelli.

Kelli released my arm and shook King's hand.

"The pleasure is mine, Sis. Doc's as good as gold, you know that, right?" he asked as he shook her hand.

Kelli nodded.

"Does she speak?' he chuckled in my direction.

"When she needs to," I laughed.

"That's what I hear," he laughed.

"Well, I'll let you guys get on with your Saturday. What were you doing here?" King asked.

"Trying to buy a new bagger. The black Street Glide," I answered.

King raised his eyebrows.

"Too damned high," I responded to his look of question.

"I hate this place. I'm going to buy a new windshield for the Road King. Probably be a hundred bucks. I hate to even spend that here," he laughed.

"I know what you mean," I smiled.

"Doc, Sis, I'll let you two get to it. Sis, it was great to put a face with a name," he said as he looked at Kelli.

She smiled and nodded, "Nice to meet you King."

King smiled and nodded in her direction, "Doc, take care," he said as he began to walk away.

"King," I acknowledged as we pushed the door open and walked outside.

I reached into my right pocket as we walked toward the car and pulled my keys out.

"You know what I'm going to do when we get home?" I asked, shaking the keys in my hand.

She shook her head.

"I'm going to fuck you until you can't see straight. Until you're mildly retarded," I chuckled.

"Fuck-fest?" she asked, turning her head and looking up into my eyes.

I nodded slowly, "As soon as we get home. As soon as we walk in, it's on."

"Here, you drive," I said as I reached toward Kelli with the keys in my hand.

"Sir?" she said with a confused look on her face.

"Drive Kelli, you know how to drive, right?" I asked jokingly.

"You want me to drive *your* car?" she asked.

I nodded.

"You sure?" she asked.

I turned her direction and raised one eyebrow.

"It's not driving your *car* that bothers me. It's driving *you*. I know how you are, Erik. You're uncomfortable riding passenger. Yes, I'll drive. I'm glad you'll trust me to," she said as she pushed the button, unlocking the doors.

I got into the passenger seat and buckled the seatbelt. It felt odd. I tried to remember the last time I rode in the passenger seat of a vehicle. My best recollection was as a child with my mother. Kelli got into the car and buckled her seatbelt. As she started the car, I leaned toward her seat and gripped the rear of her neck in my hand with a light but firm hand.

"What, Kelli, are we going to do as soon as we get home?" I whispered into her ear. I cocked my head and looked at her face.

She smiled.

"I asked you a question," I stated.

"Fuck," she responded.

"That's correct. We're going to fuck. I'm going to shove you so full of cock you won't remember how to spell your five letter name," I muttered into her ear.

She smiled.

"You little fucker. As soon as we get home, you're going to get it. I'm going to have you dress up. Son of a bitch, baby girl - I love fucking you. You know why?" I asked, as a smirk of a smile appeared on my face.

"Because it's fun?" she said as she put the car into gear.

"Because I fucking love you," I said as I kissed her lips lightly.

As I leaned into the seat, she began to slowly pull out of the parking stall.

I smiled at the memory of my mother driving as Kelli pulled from the parking lot onto the access road. As she turned carefully onto the road leading to the on-ramp, the traffic light ahead turned to red. Slowly, she came to a stop.

Gripping the steering wheel tightly, she looked up at the light, and over toward me. She defined beauty by merely existing. By being her natural self. She smiled an evil little smile. I smiled in return.

"As soon as this light turns green, I'm going to mash this gas pedal and drive as fast as I can up that ramp," she said as she nodded her head toward the windshield.

Shit.

She turned to face the road ahead, both hands tight on the steering wheel.

I fully turned to face her. She stared straight ahead – stone faced.

I turned, lowered my head, and looked down at my seatbelt. For the sake of safety, I checked to make sure it was buckled.

"And, uhmm, I'm going to keep driving as fast as I can up the ramp and onto the highway, no matter what speed limit I reach," she turned, looked at the light, and looked at me.

I looked up from my seat belt, my heart was racing.

"I won't slow down," she paused for a few seconds.

She gripped the steering wheel with both hands.

"There's two...well, let's say *three* things that'll get me to slow down, Erik. We'll either wreck, or get arrested. Or uhhmm, you're going to make me cum," she turned toward me and smiled as she reached down and unbuttoned her pants.

Incapable of speaking, I stared at her in awe.

This sounded way too familiar.

"Speak English?" she asked, her eyes squinted.

"Kelli, you better not..." I didn't finish speaking when the light turned green.

She gripped the wheel and mashed the gas pedal. The car lunged forward as the exhaust screamed a tone reminiscent of a street race.

"God damn it Kelli!" I screamed as I reached for my seat belt.

The exhaust roared as the car quickly accelerated.

She hit second gear and the car jolted, sliding sideways for an instant before the slip control activated.

SCOTT

The exhaust tone grew louder as the car increased speed; already well above the speed limit.

"Kelli, if you wreck this fucking car..."

She hit third gear and smiled as the car blazed up the on-ramp toward the highway. The sound from the exhaust overcame the sound from the already loud music.

Without concern, she turned up the volume to the radio.

Paul Thorn, Ain't Love Strange played as she hit fourth gear and swerved onto the highway, merging *through* traffic. *This crazy little fucker can drive.*

As I leaned into her lap, I turned and looked at the speedometer.

135 miles an hour.

Jesus fucking Christ.

I had no idea what I was getting into when I asked her to loosen up and be herself.

No idea.

Chapter Two

*E*RIK. Time passes and things change. Today, change is good. Change is welcome, and change is allowing me to live a life most people only dream of.

I hung the talisman from the nail and leaned back on the ladder to take a look. I straightened it a little and looked again. Standing on the floor it would be barely visible, and impossible to reach without a ladder. I stepped down the ladder and onto the floor.

It hung directly over our bed, and right in the center of where the headboard was. I nodded affirmatively and picked up the ladder.

As I carried the ladder down the stairs, I almost lost my footing half way down. The steps were wooden and did not have any covering, carpeting, or other means of providing a surface suitable for walking in socks.

I placed the ladder in the storage room and walked into the entry hall.

"Baby Girl!" I screamed up the stairs.

"On my way," a muffled voice came from the upstairs bedroom.

I heard footsteps running across the upper floor and then the sound of what appeared to be a herd of cattle coming down the stairs. The clamor coming down the steps was followed by a quick *thud*, and a *whumpity, whumpity, whumpity, whump*.

Kelli's body hit the floor at the base of the steps.

"Son of a bitch, are you alright?" I asked as I turned her direction. She was sprawled out at the base of the steps in a short black dress, most of which was around her neck. From her boobs down, she was bare.

"Fucking fuck. Yeah, I'm fine," she said as she stood up, "my heel broke or something. I hate those steps, they're slippery."

SCOTT

I reached around her to give her a hug, "You sure you're okay?"

"I'm fine. I need to get another pair of shoes," she said as she looked up the stairs and straightened her dress.

"Take your time," I said, laughing, "you look great, by the way."

"Thank you, sir," she said over her shoulder as she walked up the steps.

My level of satisfaction, my degree of being happy - was something that I had never experienced. My expression to Kelli about my true feelings, my burning the diary, and my honesty with myself was a cleansing process that did me more good than I ever would have guessed. My openness with my deceased parents regarding Kelli may have seemed odd to some people, but to me it was necessary. I now stood in the kitchen, the afternoon of our house warming party, as happy as I have ever been in my life.

I felt complete. Whole. Satisfied.

Kelli Parks was not an *avenue* to happiness or a means of *making* me happy. Kelli *was* my happiness. Kelli told me at Il Vicino one day that she was *weak for me*. I now realized that I, too, was weak for her. We were certainly a match for each other in many respects. As she came down the steps, I smiled. She had replaced the heels with black flats that had sparkles on them.

"Better?" I asked.

"Much. My hip is bruised. Well, it *feels* bruised," she said as she turned to look over her shoulder.

"Come here. Turn around," I said as I rotated my hand in a circle.

She turned around so her back would face me. I lifted her dress and inspected her skin for marks.

"There's a spot *here*," I said as I poked a rash on her thigh.

"And *here*," I poked a scrape on her right butt cheek.

"That's it?" she asked.

I held her dress higher and looked around her. I raised my left hand and slapped her left butt cheek as hard as I could without knocking her over.

"FUCK!" she screamed as she stumbled on her feet.

"Hand print. There's a hand print on your left cheek" I added, laughing.

"Fucker," she said as she turned around. She rubbed her butt as she smiled.

"Kelli, before everyone gets here, I want to say a few things. Come here," I said as I walked into the living room.

She followed me in to the living room, and sat on the couch beside me.

"There's going to be a few hundred people here. Some over time, but a lot at once," I said as I placed my hand on her leg.

She nodded.

"We've come a long way, baby girl. A long damned way. I'm happy about it. You know you mean the world to me, right?"

She looked at me, and nodded sharply a few times, smiling.

"Nobody could ever replace you. You're weak for me, and I'm weak for you. We're perfect for each other. I feel as if living one simple day without you would strangle me, Kelli. I don't even want to think about it. Don't mistake me being weak for you as me being or becoming weak, I am far from it. Does that make sense?" I asked.

"I think so," she answered.

"Listen. You're perfect for me. And I am not afraid to admit it. I told you before, and I will tell you again. I will take care of you. For all of what is forever. You, in turn, take care of me. Do you understand?" I asked.

She nodded.

"Kelli?" I reached for her neck, and placed my hand around her neck, squeezing lightly and playfully.

My squeezing her neck actually made her comfortable and settled her down. She slumped into my hand and leaned toward me, resting her head on my bicep.

"Yes sir?" she asked.

"Do you understand?" I asked.

Her eyes now closed, she nodded. I massaged her neck in my hand and firmed my grip a little.

"Kelli, I don't know if you noticed, but when we were at the Harley dealer, I said *we* when referencing buying the motorcycle. *We* offered this. *We* will take it. *We* this, *we* that. I did that for a reason. Did you notice?" I asked.

Her eyes closed, she nodded, "Yes, I did. I liked it."

"Kelli, there is no longer a *you* and an *I*. We are an *us*. This house? This house is not *mine*. I want you to understand, this house is *ours*. When these people come, this is *our* home. Ours. You tell people this is our house, and you do so proudly. I will do the same. Okay?" I asked as I massaged her neck.

She nodded slowly, her head rubbing against my bicep. Her long black hair draped onto my lap.

"Are you ever going to disappoint me, Kelli?" I asked.

She opened her eyes and turned her head toward me.

"Never," she responded, "never."

She scrunched her brow and looked at me as if I asked her to jump off of a cliff.

"Okay. I will not disappoint you either. You know, earlier, when we were going at it, that the sex can be rough sometimes. It doesn't mean I don't care for you or that I am mad. You know that, right?"

SCOTT

She turned to face me fully. I let go of her neck.
"When we got back from the Harley shop?" she asked.
I nodded.
"Pffffttt. Let me say something please," she said.
"Okay," I responded, "please do."
"You know what you have to do to get me wet? To get me *soaking*. Walk. Pick something up with those sexy hands. Bend over and pick something up. Smile. Cut your sandwich in half. Open my car door. Laugh. Wake up. Take a drink out of your water bottle. Kick Tommy's or his idiot uncle's ass. Name it. I want to fuck you always. Erik I'm so serious. Always. You say you own me. You do. And please, never stop reminding me, I love it. But this pussy," she paused and pointed between her legs.

"It isn't mine anymore. It's *yours*. I just carry it around for you until you need it. I used to masturbate half a dozen times a day. Since I met you, not at all," she paused and shook her head.

"You may think you're going to out fuck me, make me slap the wall three times or whatever. It's *not* going to happen. Ever. Erik, I love you. And I will never intentionally be disrespectful *toward* you. I will never disrespect you to others either," she inhaled a slow breath and looked up at the ceiling.

I started to speak.
She held her index finger in the air.
"You could fuck me until I was unconscious. Call an ambulance, and have me hauled to the hospital for a worn out pussy and dehydration. When the paramedics are checking me out and giving me an I.V., you know what I'll be wishing for?" she asked.

I smiled and shook my head, knowing where she was headed with this.

"I would be wishing you were in the ambulance fucking me for the ride to the hospital. You will never out-fuck me. *Ever.* We don't need to talk about this anymore, but you should *know* this about me by now. I like fucking you. I like it a lot. I'd rather be fucking you than talking to you, that's for damned sure. Most of the time, anyway," she laughed as she finished speaking.

"Now?' I asked.
"Fucking," she smiled.
"When everyone gets here?" I asked.
"Fucking," she giggled and started rocking back and forth on the sofa.
"At the restaurant? Mall? Car? On the steps? Kitchen? Oh, here you go, at your father's house? Dealership on the sales floor?" I smiled.

"Fucking, fucking, fucking, fucking, fucking, and fucking. Is that right?" she counted on her fingers and bounced in the sofa cushion.

"Nope, one more. *Fucking*," she laughed, shaking her hands at me, her fingers extended and spread apart.

"Fuck me," she said as she stood up.

She straightened her dress, raised her eyebrows, and waited.

The sound of a car coming up the driveway interrupted our conversation. She turned and looked out the window toward the driveway.

"It's Heather and Teddy," she squealed as she turned and ran toward the door.

Neither of them had been here since we moved in to the house. They had helped us move in, but decided not to come back until we were settled and had our party. I hadn't expected them *this* early; but knowing Teddy, he wanted to help set up the party as much as possible.

Kelli stood at the door, holding it open. I suspected as she normally sees Teddy and Heather three or four times a week, she wasn't as excited to see *them* as she was to have them see her – *at her new home*.

"So, did you get all of your furniture..." Heather started to ask as she walked in the door.

She and Kelli both squeaked as Kelli moved from the doorway. They both turned and ran into the living room, squealing and looking at the furniture.

"Well, fuck. Guess we ain't huggin' no more. Sis, my ass. Bone shoulda named you something else. Maybe *ass-hat*. Yep, ass-hat woulda been better," Teddy winked at me as he walked through the door.

Kelli turned around and ran toward Teddy, jumped and wrapped herself around him as he stood in the entrance. Her legs were wrapped around his thighs, and her arms around his shoulders.

"Sum bitch, Kelli. Now *that's* a hug," Teddy said as Kelli let go and fell to the floor.

"Doc, how the hell are ya, brother?" Teddy said as he walked my direction.

We shook hands and I hugged him.

"Love what you done to the place," he laughed as he looked around, "where you keep the cold beer?"

"Kegs are out in the shop. They delivered them this morning before we went to the Harley dealer," I answered.

"Couldn't make it work, huh?" Teddy asked, shaking his head.

"No, too damned high. Twenty-two on a Street Glide. And it was a 2013," I responded.

"Why fuck. He's a fuckin' mental midget. I hate that fuckin' shop.

SCOTT

You know they fucked up Buster's bike in 2010. Fried the motor before he got off the lot. Know what they told him?" he asked.

I'd heard the story of Buster having the motor on his bike rebuilt a hundred times. He no more than got out of the dealership and half a mile up the highway before it flew apart. The dealership did nothing to assist in the repairs of their work. They responded that it was a high performance motor, and they didn't warrant high performance motors.

"No, what?" I asked.

"Fuckers told him it was a hi-po motor and they didn't repair hi-po motors. *Why fuck fellas, you're the ones that made it a hi-po.* It was bone stock when it went in, came out a hi-po. I'm afraid I'd have had someone's head on a stick over that deal," he shook his head and looked around the house.

"Love the place, Doc," he nodded his head as he looked around the room.

Kelli and Heather ran from the living room up the stairs.

"I just had Kelli go to that place on Rock Road and pick out whatever she wanted that day you and I went to the bar last week. They delivered everything that afternoon," I said as I looked around.

"Surprised your weird ass let her do that. You're odd as fuck, Doc. Especially when it comes to houses," Teddy laughed.

"Now where's that beer?" he asked again.

"I have a bunch of imports in the fridge and in the shop," I said, pointing into the kitchen.

"Do I look like I drink imports?" Teddy said as he raised one eyebrow.

"We're going to the garage," I screamed up the stairs as Teddy and I walked past the stairway.

"Okay," a half audible tone came from upstairs.

"Man, them girls is something else, huh?" Teddy asked as we walked outside.

"Jesus, Kelli is opening up. She's a different person since we moved in here," I laughed.

"Shit, Doc. Act like you didn't know that little gal was a handful. That's why you like her. She's gonna give you a run for your damned money," he chuckled as he slapped me on the arm.

"Shit fuck, Doc," he said as he opened the door to the garage.

"What?" I asked.

"God damn, you buy two lifts?" he asked as he looked around the shop.

"Yep. I had them delivered a few days ago. Kind of nice having a place to store the bikes for the winter. I figured I could tinker with them on the lift for off-season. Figured I'd buy that Glide. Fucking bastards," I said, thinking about the over-priced Harley dealer.

"I'd like to light that place on fire, I'm tellin'ya," Teddy shook his head as he opened the refrigerator and grabbed a beer.

"You and I agree on that one," I laughed.

"Band gonna be back there?" he asked as he pointed to the rear of the shop.

The house that we had purchased had an attached garage. Additionally, it had a detached garage or shop beside the driveway that was forty feet wide and sixty feet long. It was large enough to have farm equipment in, but there was no need. It served me perfectly to keep my motorcycles in, and have an occasional party.

"Yeah. I figured they'd get set up in the rear of the shop. Hell, it's still eighty degrees outside, we can open the doors and let them play," I responded.

"Get that kid from down town? Timmy Jonas?" he asked.

"Yeah. Kelli talked to him. He lived there in her building, and she didn't even realize it. He's good to go," I said.

"Well brother, should be a good time. So, you settled in yet?" he asked.

"We've got it all moved in. Hell, Kelli has every damn thing in place. She's amazing like that," I responded as we walked toward the rear of the shop.

"No, I mean having a girl live with ya, Doc. You adjusting all right?" he asked as he took a drink from his bottle of beer.

I stopped and looked around the shop. My feelings should be difficult to explain, but my response came easily as we walked together.

"Teddy, I love that woman. Being with her is where I belong. It may seem strange to you, or for you to hear it, but it's true. Living here with her has allowed me to exhale. For once in my life, I feel like I can let my guard down. I can be myself around her. Hell, I don't even know if I know who I really am. I think I'm finding out," I shook my head and laughed.

"I'm doing and saying things that I never would have guessed. I'm not trying to impress her, or win her heart; hell that's done. But I see myself and what I am doing - it just seems strange. Strange and kind of comforting," I stopped and turned to Teddy.

"Doc, right is right. And wrong's wrong. Pretty much. So, if it feels right, it is. Guy don't need him a sheep skin from college to know that. If it's right, let it be. Don't seem weird to me. Hell, don't you dare say a word, but I'm thinking about asking Heather to marry me," Teddy said as he rubbed his beard with his left hand.

"Holy shit, Teddy. Well..." I paused and thought.

"*Well what?* Don't matter, Doc. Don't matter if it's been a month since I met her, six months, or six years. It's either right or wrong. There's always what we think and then there's what we *know*. I know this - I love that woman. Ain't much sense in trying to tell myself anything otherwise. I look at it this way - it's my damned *job* to keep her happy. Marryin' a girl is making her dream come true. So if it's inevitable, just as well get it over with," he said as looked down at the floor.

"I was just thinking, sorry. I agree with ya, brother. It's no shock to me. Hell I'm happy for you if you two get married. It'll sure make Kelli jealous," I looked at the floor and thought of things changing between Teddy and I.

"Like how I did that?" he raised his eyebrows and took a drink of beer.

"What's that?" I asked.

"Used a big word for ya," he responded.

I squinted and shook my head, not quite understanding his question.

"*Inevitable*. Used it a minute ago. Was kinda proud of myself. Hell, Heather has me readin' shit damned near every night on a Kindle. Crazy little girl bought me my own. I'm gonna try and use one new word a day – well, might not be *new*, but it'll be new to *me* using it," he laughed.

I shook my head and smiled. Before I could say a word, he spoke.

"*Circumspect*. That's a sum bitch there. Had it in a book I was reading last night. Had to look that fucker up," he tipped his bottle up.

"Being aware of all the shit around ya, Doc. Being aware. Circumspect. Hell, I'm circumspect," he laughed.

"Reading books is good for you, Teddy," I laughed, "who says bikers are a bunch of dummies."

"Hell I never heard that one before," Teddy laughed.

"Grab a few beers, let's go inside," I said, wondering what the girls were doing.

As we turned to walk to the refrigerator, I noticed the girls walking through the door into the shop.

"I'm so excited, how much longer," Kelli asked.

"For what?" Teddy screamed across the shop as we walked toward the door.

"Till everyone gets here," she laughed as she walked toward me.

"Hell Sis, party has been cancelled. Didn't you hear," he laughed.

"Timmy is gonna show up, he said he was. He and I will have our own party," Kelli laughed.

"Timmy Jonas is comin'?" Teddy asked with a surprised tone, "hell, he's fuckin' famous. Who rounded him up?"

"I did," Kelli answered proudly as she raised her finger in the air.

As Teddy hugged Heather and reached into the refrigerator, he spoke.

"Call em' back Doc, tell em to come. This mother-fucker's gonna be a party to remember," Teddy stated.

"*Our* party," Kelli said as she put her arms around my waist.

"Ours," I confirmed.

I liked the sound of that.

Ours.

Chapter Three

GENE. "Well, if I asked you to guess, what's your best guess?" I asked.

"Hard to say, Mr. Parks. Could be six months. Might be three weeks. It's just a number that we can't define. There are no assurances. With the dialysis, maybe six months," the doctor responded.

"That an educated guess, Doc?" I asked.

"Yes sir. I wish I had better news. And with your age and your blood type, a donor is pretty close to being out of the question," he said.

Doctors don't sugar coat a damned thing.

When I was in the military, I always wondered what would happen if I was shot. It was a constant fear of mine. My blood type being AB negative made me a candidate for dying if there was ever a circumstance that I needed blood and needed it fast. As I stepped out of the gown and began to get dressed, I wondered if any amount of money could buy me a kidney.

"Doc, hold up a minute," I said as I raised my hand.

"Doc, you know I have more money than most. Does that help?" I asked, hopeful of an affirmative answer.

"It helps, Gene. But, having your blood type, and at your age, it's just...well, there are people that have waited *years*. You don't have years. I'm sorry we don't have better answers for you," he said as he looked up from the floor.

"Anything else?" he asked.

I shook my head slowly from side to side, "No sir."

I had lost one kidney just before Kelli was born. I was damned near forty years old at the time. They attributed the loss from being exposed to Agent Orange during the war. They explained then that I may lose the other at any time. I liked to imagine the chemical company that made Agent Orange never suspected that it would kill all of the foliage in the jungle but not kill the soldiers, sailors and Marines that were in the jungle.

That God forsaken war was going to kill me one way or the other.

"Thanks, Doc," I said as he opened the door.

Having between a few weeks and six months to live puts things into an entirely new perspective. What was important now seemed unimportant. What isn't or wasn't important all of a sudden becomes so.

My mind raced.

Life is a mystery that will go unsolved. It is not to be figured out, it's to be lived to the best of our abilities. I have no regrets and nothing to be ashamed of. To me, I have solved life.

Being without regret.

Receiving fire in Vietnam never made me *worry* about dying. In the war, death was something that crossed my mind from time to time, but it wasn't a constant thought or concern. Now, having the knowledge that death was inevitable was not something that set very well in my stomach.

I walked to the bathroom and placed my hands on my thighs. As I bent my knees and lowered myself to the floor, I began to cry.

Chapter Four

*K*ELLI. "To make a long story short, we didn't come here to get sober. After this one, we're going to take a little break," Timmy Jonas said into the microphone.

"This one is for Doc's baby girl," his voice crackled through the speakers as he began to play Stony Larue's Long Black Veil.

"Shit Doc, you gotta dance to this one," Teddy said as he grabbed Heather's hand.

Erik placed his right hand over my shoulder, and we began to dance. As we did, Teddy and Heather joined in beside us. Dancing with Erik seemed surreal. I never would have guessed my life would come to a point that something like this would be happening to me.

I was in love.

In love with a man that loved me back. *Just like it was in the book.*

Trying to make sense of everything was overwhelming and I wondered when something was going to go wrong. Some part of my life had to fall apart sooner or later; this was too good to be true. Erik and I went from meeting each other to this in six months. I was living in a dream, and I never wanted it to end.

Erik moved my hair away from my ear and his mouth moved close enough I could feel his breath.

"Who baby girl?" he whispered into my ear.

As we danced, I poked him in the chest with my index finger.

"I like to hear you say it. Who baby girl?" he asked again.

I love it when he asks me this.

"You do," I responded.

"That's right baby girl, I do," he whispered into my ear.

As the song ended, Erik placed his hands on each side of my face and kissed me on the lips.

"I love you, Kelli," he said.

"I love you back," I said.

"We'll be back after a short break, thank you," the singer said.

I don't know how many people had shown up at our party, but the house was full, the shop was full, and the yard was full. There were motorcycles everywhere, and cars and trucks that lined each side of the street. Erik said a few hundred would show up. It seemed like many more than that. All of these people coming to see us made me happy and nervous. Erik seemed like he didn't really care.

"Hi Jake," I said as Jake walked up to beside where we were standing.

"Sis," Jake nodded his head and smiled.

Jake was so cute. I wish he had a girlfriend. He was shorter than everyone else Erik rode with. He said he was five foot ten, but Erik said he was a stretch at five foot nine. He was stocky and had short kind of curly hair.

"Doc, there's a Lisa Williams and a Michelle Robinson here to see you. Said they know you from school," Jake said.

"Oh shit. Really? Hell, I was sure they wouldn't make it. Come on, Kelli. You need to meet these girls," Erik said as he grabbed my hand.

We walked out of the shop and along the sidewalk toward the house. There were picnic tables set up in the yard, and people were sitting at them talking and drinking. Our porch was lined with people. This was crazy. Crazy in a good way. As we followed Jake toward the house, two women recognized Erik and smiled. One was wearing an OSU shirt, the other was blonde and wearing a dress.

"Wow, nice place, Erik," the girl wearing an OSU shirt said.

"Lisa, I'm surprised they let you cross the border in that shirt. Oklahoma? Really?" Erik asked as he opened his arms.

She smiled and hugged him.

"There are times I miss you, Erik," she said.

Erik smiled, "I feel the same way Lisa."

"Lisa, this is my other half, Kelli Parks," Erik said as he placed his hand on my right shoulder.

I reached out and shook her hand.

"Pleased to meet you," I said.

"And Kelli, this is Michelle Robinson. Son of a bitch, Michelle, do you ever age? Damn you look great," he said as he hugged the blonde woman.

When they finished hugging, I shook the blonde woman's hand.

"I went to school with these two, Kelli. They used to crawl into my bedroom window and get advice," Erik said as he motioned toward them.

Michelle was staring at Jake.

Baby Girl III

Staring.

"Oh, I'm sorry. Ladies, this is Jake," Erik said as he pointed toward Jake.

Lisa shirt shook Jake's hand. As Jake turned to shake the hand of the blonde girl, she stared into his eyes.

"We've never formally met, I'm Michelle," she said.

She looked down at Jake's feet, slowly up toward his face, and smiled.

"Seeing a beautiful woman is like hearing a beautiful song. Once one is captured, escape is impossible until it ends," Jake said as he shook Michelle's hand.

She squeaked.

"Ma'am," Jake said to the lady in the OSU shirt as he nodded his head her direction.

Erik looked at Lisa and then at me, and smiled. He turned to Jake and Michelle, who began walking toward the garage. Jake was facing the blonde girl and talking as they walked.

The music began to play again.

"So Lisa, I'm going to guess Michelle is single?" Erik laughed.

"For now," she laughed.

"Join us for some music? We have a band in the garage," he said.

"I will in a minute, I saw Teddy up by the porch, I'm going to go talk to him, I'll catch up in a few," she said.

"Fair enough," Erik said.

"Wow, I guess Jake liked the way Michelle looked," Erik laughed as he turned toward me and smiled.

"Jake's cute," I said.

"I suppose," Erik laughed.

He put his left arm over my shoulder and we turned to walk into the garage.

As we stepped into the garage, the band was finishing a song. The singer looked up, tilted his hat back and smiled. Normally, you couldn't see his eyes. He wore a cap on his head all the time, and had it pulled down over his eyes. Normally, he didn't speak very much. He grabbed the microphone and spoke.

"R. L. Burnside tune right here. Someday Baby. Doc. Kelli. Thanks for having us," he said into the microphone.

As the music began to play, I felt a tingle. I turned and looked at Erik. Erik smiled.

"You fucked me senseless to this song," I said, remembering the day he made me cum while this song played.

I felt myself getting wet.

"Did you ask them to play it?" I asked.

Erik smiled.

The song is a fast paced blues song that's kind of sexy. Erik grabbed my shoulders in his hands and began to grind on my hips with his crotch.

Erik Ead was dirty dancing.

I felt myself beginning to melt.

People started whistling and screaming, pointing in our direction.

"*Get it, Doc*," I heard someone scream.

Erik continued to grind his hips against my thighs and hips - bending his knees and lowering himself closer to the floor, and then slowly coming back up. I was hypnotized by watching him wiggle. I placed my hands on his waist and began to grind with him.

I felt after the incident with A-Train that Erik had begun to fully trust me. When he took me to the cemetery, I knew that he did. The Erik Ead that I had been seeing for the last few weeks was the Erik Ead that I hoped would last forever. I bent my knees, lowered myself to the floor, and bit the crotch of his jeans.

"Get him, Sis," Bunny screamed.

As the song ended, we stood up straight and hugged. Several people clapped. I was uncomfortably wet. Erik moved my hair behind my ear and moved his mouth close to my face.

"You sexy little bitch. You make me want to fuck you. Always," he whispered.

"You started it," I smiled.

He leaned back, smiled, and spoke, "You're gorgeous."

"Fuck me," I whispered.

"Be careful what you wish for," he responded.

"Just like A-Train says, *if you're scared go to church*," I said, smiling.

"You're a…" he began to say.

"Mouthy little fucker," I finished.

He reached down, grabbed my hand, and began walking toward the door.

"Come on, you mouthy little shit," he said as he walked out the door, and turned to the right.

"Where are we going?" I asked, giggling.

"It's not where we're going, baby girl. It's what I'm going to do to you," he said as he walked briskly to the rear of the garage.

"What are you going to do to me?" I giggled.

"Teach you a fucking lesson," he said.

I love being in trouble with this man.

We turned and stepped behind the garage. The rear of the garage was exposed to the land behind the house. It was still somewhat visible from the side of the house, but not easily seen. Erik turned, my hand in his, and faced me. He let go of my hand and placed his hand on my neck. He pressed me against the wall. By my neck and held me there.

"Maybe you need to go to church. You scared?" he asked.

I shook my head.

"Get down on your knees, baby girl," he demanded.

I reached up and grabbed ahold of his wrist lightly. As I lowered myself to my knees, I held his hand to my throat. I reached for his zipper and unzipped his pants. As I reached inside his pants with my thumb and finger, I let go of his wrist and unbuckled his belt. I unbuttoned his pants and watched his stiff cock spring out as his pants fell open.

I grasped his cock with my right hand and began stroking it. He squeezed my neck harder and pressed my back against the wall of the garage.

"Put your hands at your sides, Kelli. Don't move them. Do not move your fucking hands for any reason. Do you understand me?" he asked.

I tried to talk, but was too excited to make myself speak. When he treated me like this, it made me a degree of excited that was unimaginable.

I nodded.

"Do you fucking understand me?" he asked sternly.

"Uh huh," was all I could mutter.

"Baby girl, I am not going to ask you again," he said as he squeezed my neck a little harder.

He pressed me harder to the wall and pushed his cock into my face, leaning into me with his hips.

I opened my mouth.

He thrust his cock forcefully into my mouth. He pushed harder, forcing it into my throat. I felt the soft head at the back of my throat. I was not ready for this. My eyes began to water. I raised my hand to wipe my face.

"Keep your fucking hands, down, Kelli," he barked.

It was becoming difficult to breathe.

He thrust himself in and out of my mouth, pressing a little harder with each stroke. He loosened his grip on my neck, pressing me with his palm into the wall of the garage.

"Do you understand me?" he asked, his cock well into my throat.

My eyes watering, I needed a breath.

He looked down and smirked as he fucked my mouth.

"Well, do you?"

He pulled his cock from my mouth.

I gasped.

"Yes, yes sir," I gasped as I took a breath.

He immediately shoved his cock back into my mouth.

"Who in the absolute fuck owns you, Kelli?" he asked as he slid his entire nine inches in and out of my throat.

He pulled his hips back. His saliva covered cock fell from my mouth.

"You. You do sir," I gasped, my face covered in my own saliva.

"Don't forget it," he said as he grabbed his cock in his hand.

"Open, Kelli. Open your fucking mouth," he demanded.

I opened my mouth.

He guided his cock into my mouth and began to work his hips back and forth.

"You, Kelli," he took a breath and looked down.

He stroked his cock in and out of my mouth twice, pressing hard as he went into my throat, forcing all of himself into my mouth.

"You're a mouthy," he shook his head.

He pressed my head hard against the wall of the garage, his balls against my lips. His hips pressed against my face. I could not breathe at all. My eyes watered and my throat convulsed. He held himself deep in my throat, pressing hard.

The music shook the garage wall. I felt the vibrations against the back of my head. I tried to concentrate on the music and forget the breathing.

"Kelli, you're a mouthy little," he paused.

Slowly, he pulled himself from my mouth.

As his cock passed my lips, I coughed and gasped.

"Fucker," I gasped, "I'm a mouthy little fucker."

Saliva dripped from my mouth and chin onto my dress.

"Yes, you are. Now stand up and turn around. Put your hands on the wall," he pointed to the wall as he shook his head from side to side.

I tried to stand as my legs shook. My bruised butt and thighs hurt. I stood and turned around, facing the wall. I could feel my wetness between my legs as I rotated. I raised my hands up even with my shoulders and pressed my palms against the wall.

"How am I going to fuck you with your panties on, Kelli? I wonder about you sometimes," he said in an irritated tone as he reached into my dress.

"Take your fucking panties off, dork. Why in the fuck are you wearing panties?" he asked.

I reached down and pushed my panties down my thighs and worked them to my calves. My pussy was soaked. I raised my feet one at a time and removed my panties. I dropped them on the ground beside me.

What was I thinking?

"I asked you a question, baby girl," he snapped.

"I don't know," I responded as I raised my hands to the wall.

"Excuse me?" he interrupted as he kicked my feet apart.

"Sir, I don't know sir," I corrected myself.

Baby Girl III

God he turns me on so much. I love this. I just love it.

My legs were shaking and my arms quivered. He lifted my dress above my waist and held it there. I felt his cock pressing against my pussy. As he slid inside of me, I gasped.

"You like that big cock, don't you, baby girl?" he asked as his right hand slipped past my shoulder to my neck.

I nodded my head excitedly and bit my lower lip.

"I asked you a question," he muttered softly.

"Yes, yes sir. I love your cock," my voice cracked when I answered.

He leaned into me. His chest was against my back, and his hips pressed against my butt.

"Your little pussy is a mess, Kelli. It's soaking wet. Did that turn you on? That little face fucking I gave you?" he whispered into my ear.

I nodded my head repeatedly and bit my lip. I felt myself begin to contract. I was going to cum hard. He excites me so much. Being behind the garage, all of the people, and feeling the wall vibrate from the music was more than I could take.

"God *damn it* Kelli," he whispered harshly into my ear.

Sometimes I think I do these things on purpose.

"Yes sir, I loved it," I responded.

He pulled his cock out of my pussy.

No, don't stop. No.

"Turn around," he demanded.

I turned to face him. As I did, he reached around the outside of my thighs, curled his hands under my butt, and picked me up. He pressed me against the wall and held me there. I reached over his shoulders and around his neck. I lifted my legs and wrapped them around him.

As I felt his cock pushing inside of me, I clenched my teeth and shook my head from side to side.

"Fuck, Kelli. I love watching you as I fill your little pussy with cock. You're a sexy little fucker," he said as he looked into my eyes.

"Mouthy fucker," I laughed as I leaned toward him to kiss him.

He bit my lip with his upper teeth as he slowly pushed his tongue into my mouth. His hands felt good under my bare butt as he fucked me. As his hips smashed his hands against my butt, I felt myself begin to contract.

Oh God, please keep that up. Right there.

He pulled his mouth from mine and looked into my eyes as he smiled.

"You going to cum for me, little girl?" he asked.

I nodded my head.

He fucked me harder. My back slapped against the wall as he

pounded my pussy with every inch of his cock. I closed my eyes and focused on the feeling of his cock inside of me.

As he continued to pound me against the wall, I began to cum.

"Erik…"

"Do it, baby girl." He said.

"Erik, I…"

I came hard.

And. I came again.

He pounded inside of me. I felt his cock swell.

Do it, you big fucker.

I felt myself begin to cum hard. I opened my eyes and pressed my mouth against his.

He began to groan into my mouth.

I bit his lip.

And he came inside of me. As he did, his hands began to lower me, my back still against the wall.

And.

I.

Came.

He lowered me to the ground and kissed me, pressing me to the wall by my shoulders. His mouth pressed hard against mine, he continued to kiss me and moan. As he slowly slipped his cock from inside of me, he pulled his mouth from mine.

"I love you, Kelli," he said.

He can never say that enough.

Never.

"Mouthy little fucker," I said.

"Mouthy little fucker," he repeated.

"I love you back," I said.

Chapter Five

*E*RIK. "If you're available, I can do it now," I said into the phone.

"Now is fine, Erik, you coming alone?" he asked.

"Yes, I am," I responded.

"Alright, looking forward to it," he said.

"See you in about ten minutes or so," I said.

"See you then," he said.

I hate talking on the phone. If I had my way, I wouldn't even have one. I realize the convenience of having them, but they irritated me. I kept mine in my pocket, and rarely pulled it out. One day, I may need to buy a better phone, but spending money on something I so detested seemed ridiculous.

I walked into the living room. Kelli was doing some workout as an image of a woman that looked half as fit and half as beautiful mirrored her actions on the television.

"Baby, I have to go take care of some business. I'll be about an hour, give or take. I'm taking the car," I said.

She waved at me.

I shook my head and walked toward her.

"Kiss me," I demanded.

She stood up from her crouching position and kissed me quickly.

"Okay, see you in a while," she said in a breathless voice.

"Okay," I laughed.

I walked through the kitchen into the garage. As I started the car and raised the garage door, I considered how my thoughts regarding love have changed in the last six months. Loving and being loved by me was as natural as taking a breath. I didn't even have to think about it. Kelli Parks meant more to me than anyone on this earth ever could or would. I would truly give my own life to give her just one more minute of living.

That woman just…

I smiled as I backed the car out of the driveway. As I cleared the garage and looked at the front of the house, I remembered the first time we were here. Hell, I had no idea at that time where Kelli and I would end up. Breaking into the house and fucking in the kitchen was not something that I would normally do with anyone, but she sure brought it out in me.

The more I thought about it, the more I realized how good Kelli was for me.

What void I had felt for the majority of recent years Kelli had filled fully, and she filled it naturally. As naturally as she was submissive, she was also a perfect natural fit for *me*. She fit me perfectly as woman, a respective other, and as a lover.

To think of ever trying to live without her was something that I could not make taste good in my mouth. Kelli provided for me a level of satisfaction that most men would only dream of, and she did so by simply existing.

As I pulled the car into the driveway, the reality of everything set into place. I exhaled, opened the door, and walked up the walk to the front door. Before I rang the doorbell, the door opened.

"Get your ass in here, you weren't going to ring the fucking bell were you?" he asked.

"I intended to," I responded.

"Good fucking God, son. Get in here," he said as he stepped aside to allow me into the house.

"Coffee?" he asked as soon as I stepped into the house.

"Sure," I responded.

"Cream and sugar, right?" he asked.

"Yes sir," I responded as he walked into the kitchen.

I walked and sat in the chair that I had sat in the day Kelli and I first came here. He walked into the living room and handed me the cup of coffee.

"Damn, that's good coffee," I said as I took a sip from the cup.

"Well, it's not that six dollar a cup shit you normally drink, but it ain't all bad, is it?" he asked.

"It's really pretty good," I said as I took another sip.

"Well, that was something about that Jacob kid, wasn't it?" he asked as he sat down.

"Who?" I asked, not immediately recognizing who he was speaking of.

"Alec Jacob. What do you guys call him?"

"Oh, A-Train. What about him?" I asked, thinking about A-Train's incident with the police.

Baby Girl III

"Oh, just that the cops were trying to railroad him for something that he obviously wasn't involved in," he said, trying to unsuccessfully hide a smirk of a smile.

"Yeah, I'm glad that's over," I said as I took another sip of coffee from the cup.

When it came time to stand up, Gene stood up. I admired him for doing that. I would always admire him for having done what he did for Alec. Who knows where A-Train would be now without Gene's help.

"So, to what do I owe this honor, son? Are you alright? How's that new home?" he asked.

I finished the coffee, and placed the cup on the table beside the chair. I leaned forward, took a breath, and then exhaled.

"The new home is great. Kelli is really enjoying the place. She has it decorated the way she wants it. She was exercising when I left. I imagine she's cleaning something in there now. Hell, she can't stop cleaning, she's really proud of the place. Oh, and I'm sorry you were too sick to come to the party the other day, we missed you, Gene," I said.

"Well, I was sick as a God damned dog, probably the damned flu," he said as he took a sip from his cup.

I nodded and leaned forward to the front edge of the cushion.

"So, Kelli said you were looking at buying a new bike – something she could actually ride on. Did you get one?" he asked.

"No, we tried. They were too damned high, we were ten percent apart on price," I answered, not wanting to give the exact amount of money that we disagreed on.

"Well, you know what they say about that damned place. Hell it's no secret that the guy's a crook. I could teach that asshole a little about running a dealership, you know it?" he laughed.

"I'm sure you could," I agreed.

"He's looking to sell the damned place. Wants six fucking million," Gene said, shaking his head.

"Jesus. Six?" I said, not realizing the place was for sale.

"Yep, I found out the other day at a city-wide dealership meeting. He's out of his God damned mind."

"Sounds like it," I said.

Talking to Kelli's father made me nervous. I don't know what portion of the nervousness I attached to the fact that he believed I was arrogant, and what portion I attributed to the fact that he was her father. Either way, it made me nervous to talk to him.

Nervous or not, I had some things that we needed to discuss.

"You nervous, son?' he asked as I shifted in my seat.

"Well, as a matter of fact, I am a little, yes," I responded.

The hour that we talked went far better than I expected, and was

SCOTT

a real wake-up call regarding what his thoughts, expectations, and beliefs were.

"Well, son-of-a-bitch," he placed his head in his hands and exhaled.

"You know men can talk to men about some things that they can't comfortably talk to women about. You know that, don't you?" he asked.

"Yes sir," I responded.

"Not a word of what we speak of now is to leave here. Not one damned word. This is between you and I, son. Kelli isn't to know about this," he paused, and put his hands on his knees.

I nodded.

He slowly stood from his chair and began pacing across the floor of the living room.

"Son, I don't know how well I'm gonna do this, especially now. I'm just glad you talked to me about your concerns first. Makes me feel better about spillin' my guts," he paused.

"Well, I guess I have a few things I should talk to you about. I wasn't going to, but now I am. That's just how things work. Might make this easier for me to *start* talking, but keeping going isn't going to be easy for me," he took a breath and looked in my direction.

"Keep your god damned mouth shut until I am done, alright?" he asked.

"Okay," I responded, nodding my head slowly.

"It's nothing against you, son. You have a tendency to run your mouth and interrupt a little. Not always in bad way, it's just...well, it's just. Oh, fuck it," he said as he sat down into the chair again.

I wondered what it was exactly that he wanted to talk about. We had already spoken about everything from family matters to Kelli's future, love, and everything in between.

"I know this isn't going to be easy for me, and now the more I'm thinking, I know it isn't going to be easy for you either. Just let me try to muddle through this, okay?" he asked.

"That's fine, Gene," I responded, wishing he'd just get started.

"Right around the time Kelli was born, I lost a kidney. God damned Agent Orange. Our fucking government sprayed all the foliage over there in Vietnam with the stuff. It was supposed to kill all of the plant life, give us a better idea of who was where, and keep our enemy from having a place to hide," he took a breath.

"Problem, Erik, was that the exposure of that shit to our troops caused all kinds of complications. Everyone that was within five miles of that crap when it was sprayed got cancer of some sort. Damned shame," he stood from his chair and began to pace the floor.

"So, I have lived the last twenty years with one kidney. Hell, I didn't even tell Kelli. I never wanted her to worry."

"Erik, it's my other kidney. I'm having problems with it," he said.

He walked over and sat down in his chair. Clearly, based on his nervous nature, the problems with his kidney were serious - at least serious to him. I tried to act relaxed and wait for what else he had to say.

"Dialysis. They've started dialysis, and it'll be three or four days a week. My blood type is AB negative, and with my age…with my age…I'm not valuable…"

His forearms on his knees, he looked down at the floor. He raised his hands, and placed his palms on either side of his face.

And he began to sob.

I stood and walked toward his chair. I reached over and placed my hand on his shoulder as he continued to cry.

"Gene, whatever this is, we can…"

"Three weeks to six months," his voice cracked as he spoke.

"Three weeks to six months of what? Dialysis?" I asked, confused.

When he responded, I felt as if someone plunged a knife into my heart.

"That's how long I've got…" he paused.

"To live," he said as he looked up.

The reality of it all sank into my being.

This man was dying.

Most people live their lives concerned with what they own, where they live, and who they know. How much money they make, what they drive, and the clothes that they wear are more important than living a life of worth.

I stood over Kelli's father full. Full of anger, grief, sorrow, and of hope. Hope that I could trade all that I had and all that I would ever have to buy him more time on this earth. I attempted to swallow through what proved to be a throat that was full of love.

"Gene…" I paused and tried to maintain my composure.

He continued to cry. It had become uncontrollable for him. He was sobbing.

I knelt down on both knees, and placed my hand on his shoulder. I turned my head and wiped the tears from my face with my free hand. Gene needed strength, comfort, and hope. For the life of me, I could not stop crying. The thought of Kelli losing her father was more than I wanted to accept right now.

Especially now.

I turned back to him as tears streamed down my face.

"Gene…"

He lifted his head from his hands and through his sobs, tried to speak.

SCOTT

"Erik, make me a promise. You're a man of honor, make me a promise," he asked, his hands shaking and face soaked with tears.

"Anything," I stuttered.

"Take care of my little girl, Erik." He said as he stood.

He wiped his face on his forearm, looked up at the ceiling and he screamed. He literally screamed the loudest most nerve racking howl I had ever heard. He shook his head, lowered his gaze, and looked at me.

"I'm alright now," he paused.

"Son-of-a-bitch, I lost it there for a few minutes. I just needed to clear my head. I used to do that in the war - a good blood curdling scream. We'd be on the river taking fire, and I manned the machine gun. I'd fucking scream and let 'em have it. It made it all make sense. Sometimes a good loud scream is all that it takes to clear the mind and soul of a mile of grief. Wipe those tears off of your face, son. You look like a damned fool," he said as he pointed to my face and smiled.

I turned the other direction and wiped my face. His strength and his situation caused me to choke as I wiped my tears.

I started to cry again.

I gazed down at the floor, and placed both hands over my face and wiped my tears.

This was useless.

I looked up, still rubbing my eyes.

And I screamed.

Chapter Six

*T*HE BONE. "Listen up," I paused and bit my cigarette between my teeth.

"You with the mouth, talking in the back. Turn around," I cupped my hands around my cheeks and screamed.

"Where you from?" I asked, pulling the cigarette from my lips.

"The Patriot Guard," he responded.

"Well, I appreciate all you fellas stand for. I don't know how you do it when you're having a meeting, but when we have 'em, we have one person speak and everyone else listens. I'm the speaker, so turn around and pay attention, alright?" I lowered the tone of my voice a little as I spoke.

"Fellas, we have an issue. A concern. I have no idea if we can resolve it, but I'm sure going to give it all *my* attention," I scanned the room to make sure all eyes were on me.

I looked down at the floor and took a drag from my cigarette.

"Doc's girl, Sis. Her father is dying. Dying as we speak. He has from a week or so to maybe a few weeks to live. His kidney is failing and he only has one. He lost the other in the war. His blood type is AB negative, which is really rare," I exhaled and took another drag from the cigarette.

"He needs a donor. There's no amount of money that we can raise to fix this. A Poker run isn't going to fix anything. A fundraiser isn't the answer. One person is needed," I patted Doc on the shoulder and exhaled the smoke.

"One person is needed to donate a kidney. Is there anyone that's AB negative and wants to donate a kidney?" I asked.

No one said a word.

SCOTT

I spit my cigarette on the floor and smashed the butt with the toe of my boot.

"I ain't looking to go into a bunch of detail, but we *owe* this man. He really sacrificed a lot for the sake of this club, he's one hell of a man, and he's all that Kelli has for a parent," I said.

People softly talked to each other, but no one spoke up.

"Anyone AB negative?" I asked.

Silence.

"Listen up, fellas. We can't put up flyers. We can't go about conventional ways of asking around. Hell, it probably wouldn't even be a good idea to ask around with your family. The problem is that Sis' father doesn't want her to know he's sick. Not yet. So, this conversation stays here," I said, pointing to the floor.

Not a word from the crowd.

"One hundred mother-fuckers in here and not one is AB negative?" I asked.

Silence.

"Well, I guess that's it. If you don't know your blood type, go get checked. If you find that you're AB negative, and you're willing to step up and make a sacrifice, call Doc or call me," I paused and looked at the floor.

"I want to tell you fellas something I probably shouldn't. Just a while ago, we had a member in trouble. Bad. Doc's girl, Kelli...Sis stepped in to help. She made a huge sacrifice. She took one hell of a risk. When I asked her why she did it, what motivated her, I was shocked at what she told me," I pulled my pack of cigarettes from my pocket.

I put a cigarette in my mouth, lit it, and pushed the pack back into my pocket.

"When it comes time to make a difficult decision, we are defined by the decisions that we make. When the collective wisdom of the universe says to shut up, yet you believe that it is time to stand up," I took a drag from the cigarette and paused, making sure all eyes were on me.

"*Stand up*," I paused again, exhaling the smoke.

"The pride that you gain will fuel you for a lifetime, and your character will never again be in question," I bit the cigarette in my teeth, and squinted as the smoke rose into my eyes.

"That's what she said. One hell of a woman right there, fellas. This ain't easy fellas. Life ain't easy. This is a sacrifice. A decision like this will define the character of a man, that's for sure," I looked around the shop.

"I need someone to *stand up*," I took a drag from the cigarette and pulled it from my lips.

"That's all I got fellas," I said as I clapped my hands together.

Baby Girl III

I turned to Doc.

"Doc, all we can do is ask. Fact of the matter is probably ain't no one here AB negative. And, if there was, ain't no one gonna want to give one of their kidneys to a sixty five year old man. It's a motherfucking shame," I said.

As people started walking out of the shop, Teddy walked up to Doc and I.

"Crash," I said as he walked up.

"I can tell you one fuckin' thing and it's a for sure," Teddy growled.

"What's that, Crash?" I asked.

"If I was AB negative, you'd be cuttin' mine out right here and now. Hell, I couldn't spill it out quick enough. I'd have you runnin' it to the damned hospital on the back of that bike in a beer cooler," he said.

"Appreciate ya, Crash," Erik said.

"So, he's pretty bad, Doc?' I asked.

Erik nodded his head slowly.

"He's as strong and as mean of a man as I have ever met, but it's beyond that, Bone. He's dying. Hell, his skin color is…" his voice faded.

I patted him on the shoulder.

"I know you ain't a religious man, Doc. My family will be praying for all of ya," I said as I pulled my cigarettes form my pocket.

"Doc, you know I would," Jake said as he walked up to the group.

Doc looked up.

"I know you would, Jake. I appreciate that. So what's the skinny between you and Michelle?" Erik asked.

"Who's Michelle?" I asked, turning toward Jake.

"Friend of mine from high school. Jake ran off with her at the party," Erik said.

"God damn, kid. What are you, twenty?" I asked as I lit a cigarette.

"I'm twenty-seven. Well, not yet, but here pretty soon," Jake said.

"Hell, if she's Doc's age, she's gotta be a dime over ya, kid. Probably thirty-six or so," I laughed.

"She looks good, boss," Erik said.

"Big titties?" I asked as I took a drag from my cigarette.

"I don't care how old she is, I like her. She's nice, and her boob size is not up for discussion," Jake snapped.

Erik raised his eyebrows and nodded.

Everyone except Jake laughed.

"Bun, Train," Erik said.

SCOTT

"Well hell, fellas, it's a fucking party. Bunny, you get that exhaust on your bike?" I asked, trying to change the subject.

People continued walked through the shop to the front, starting their bikes, and leaving.

"Yes sir, last week. Sounds like it ought to. Had to run to Harley to get a bracket. Hundred nine bucks. Bastards," Easter said.

"I swear. I tried to buy a Glide out there last week. They wanted twenty-two. I offered twenty. They refused me," Erik said.

"2013 or 2014 model," A-Train asked.

"2013. Black one on the showroom floor. New left over model," Erik said.

"Crazy assholes. Shit a '13 can be bought in Tulsa for that, Doc. Go to Tulsa," Easter said.

"Probably will, Bun. Just trying to get it here," Erik said.

"Well, I got to get, fellas. I got some shit to get done," Easter said.

"See ya, Bunny," I said as I slapped him on the shoulder.

"Wonder if Bunny is ever going to finish that sleeve on his arm," Erik asked as Easter walked to the garage door.

"Probably about the same time you finish yours," I answered.

"Fellas, I want a drink. The atmosphere here is repugnant," Teddy said.

"What did you just say?" Train asked.

"Said I was thirsty," Teddy answered.

"No, you said *repugnant*. I know you did. My left ear is still good, I heard ya, plain as day. Repugnant," Train said.

I turned to Teddy.

"Means disgusting. Offensive to taste or feeling," Teddy responded, smiling.

"What..." I started.

"The fuck?" A-Train finished my thought.

"Been readin'. Heather bought me a Kindle. I been looking up a word or two a day. I'm makin' my vocabulary a richer, more powerful tool. Now, let's go get a fuckin' drink. Peaks is callin' me. Coldest beer in town," Teddy said.

"Shit, sounds good to me," I said.

"Fellas?" I asked.

Everyone nodded.

"Sounds good to me," A-train said.

"Me too," said Jake.

"Well, let's lock this bastard up and head out. Jake, get the doors," I said as I turned to walk to the front of the shop.

Erik has made so much progress in the last few months. His meeting Kelli was the best thing that ever happened to him. The thought of him losing her father made me wonder how it would affect him and what difference it might make in how he viewed life. He was a strange person to try to figure out. He never really spoke about how he felt.

This time, I was afraid he didn't have to speak.

Gene's pain was Erik's pain.

And Gene was dying.

Chapter Seven

KELLI. "If you fall off of that ladder, I will beat your little skinny ass, woman," Erik screamed.

"I know how to climb a ladder," I said as I stepped of off of the ladder and onto the roof.

"Be careful, I don't want to have to haul you to the hospital," he said as he walked my direction.

"I'm sure footed. Yoga, P90X, kick boxing. I'm good to go," I reassured him.

"Well, this roof is steep, so just be careful," he said again.

"Why are you doing this now?" I asked.

It was exciting to have a house, and to have Erik putting up the Christmas lights, but I wanted him to be fucking me. The thought of spending Christmas with Erik in our own house was almost more than I could take. I walked toward him and slipped as I walked. I leaned forward and pushed myself back up by pressing my hands on the roof. I hoped that he didn't see me.

"*I saw that*, you damn near slid of the roof," he said as he faced the other direction.

Sometimes I felt that Erik had eyes in the back of his head. He never let me get away with *anything*.

"I wanna fuck," I said as he pulled the string of lights across the roof.

"Well, baby girl, I'm putting up these lights while the weather is warm. I'm excited to spend Christmas with my family. I haven't had a Christmas with family in a long time. *You* are my family, and it excites me," he said over his shoulder as he walked to the corner of the roof.

"It excites me too," I admitted.

I felt bad for not thinking about Erik and Christmas. Christmas was a still few months away, but it would be here before we knew it. Christmas with Erik would be the best Christmas ever. Spending Christmas with someone like him would be perfect. I could sit in the street in a cardboard box with Erik and be happy. Having him in my life was all that mattered.

"I wanna fuck really bad," I said as he walked my direction again. He was wearing jeans, boots, and a black tee shirt.

Something about this house turned me on. Every time I took time to think about it, I remembered the day that we broke in when we left the airport. Erik fucking me in the kitchen and licking my pussy on the kitchen counter was so exciting. Now, just standing in the kitchen made me wet. Standing on the roof and watching Erik drag the strings of lights across the roof in his tee shirt made me wetter.

"Well baby girl, I want to fuck too, but it's going to be about thirty minutes or better before I'm done here," he said as he walked up to me.

He held the string of lights in one hand, and a staple gun in the other. He stopped in front of me and shook his head lightly from side to side.

"What?" I asked.

"You. You're fucking beautiful, Kelli. Simply fucking beautiful," he said.

I loved it when he told me things like that. It made me feel like I actually was beautiful. He certainly didn't *need* to tell me, but he did. It meant more that way. The fact that he already had me, knew he wasn't going to lose me, and said it anyway – it just made it that much more perfect.

It made him perfect.

"Bad," I said.

"Excuse me?" he said as he bent over to staple the lights to the edge of the roof.

"I want to fuck you really bad," I repeated.

"I gathered that, baby girl. You've told me three times," he looked over his shoulder and laughed.

I worked my way to the upper portion of the roof. Our bedroom was on the second floor, and where the roof from the bedroom met the roof from the rest of the house, the two formed a valley. It looked like a safe place to sit. I leaned forward and walked up toward the bedroom window.

"Be careful, I don't want you to fall off," he said as I walked up the roof.

"I gathered that. You've told me three times," I responded.

"Twice, you little..."

"Mouthy little fucker," I giggled.

Baby Girl III

"You do want fucked, don't you?" he asked as he walked back toward the center of the roof.

I nodded my head once sharply as he made eye contact.

"Well, as soon as I am done," he said as he grabbed another strand of lights.

"You're gonna get it," he said.

"Promises, promises," I laughed.

Watching Erik do anything made me horny as hell. I could watch him write a note for the grocery store and it made me wet. I suppose that's the difference between *loving* someone and just *fucking* them. The connection between Erik and I was so strong that witnessing him in his day-to-day activities was satisfying in itself.

I needed nothing more than to know that he was pleased with me being in his life.

And for him to fuck me.

To *prove* it.

The sun felt good. There was virtually no wind, which was uncommon for Kansas and certainly uncommon for autumn. The sky was clear, and it was about 80 degrees. I laid into the valley of the roof and closed my eyes.

The smell of the flowers was perfectly sweet. It wasn't overwhelming. It was enough that you raised your head and opened your eyes a little wider to try and catch another sniff of them before they were gone.

I looked around the room.

Pedals from the roses were everywhere. The entire floor was rose pedals. I looked down at my dress, which was gathered on the floor at my feet. I must have fallen asleep. My bare feet felt cool on the rose pedals that lined the floor.

Late.

I'm going to be late.

I stood up and shook my head. I could hear the music.

Where is my father?

Isn't my dad supposed to be here to take me? I looked around the room. The music got louder and louder. I rubbed the sleep from my eyes and opened the door. I looked both directions down the hallway. The music seemed louder to the right.

I turned and ran to the right, following the sound of the music. I lifted my dress and ran down the stairs. I took two steps with each leap, trying to make up time. As my bare feet reached each step, I was grateful that I had forgotten my shoes. No one would notice with my dress on the floor covering my feet.

As I reached the bottom of the stairs, I inhaled a deep breath. The music seemed to be coming from the doors on my right. I tiptoed across the tile floor to the doors. As the music played, I opened one of the doors a few inches and peeked inside.

Almost everyone was there. Erik, Teddy, Bone, Shakey, A-Train, Jake, Heather, Amy, Donna, Chris, Emily, and Debb. I looked to the right and scanned the room. My father was not anywhere to be seen. A crow flew through the church and landed on top of the organ.

The music got louder.
And louder.
"Kelli," someone screamed.
"Kelli," the voice came again, louder.
"Kelli," it grew even louder.
Someone grabbed my arm and pulled. I pulled back, and turned to see who it was.

"Kelli, wake up. I'm done. Are you okay," Erik asked.

I opened my eyes and looked around. I felt lost. I rubbed my eyes and looked up at Erik.

"I'm done baby girl," he said, standing over me with a staple gun in his hand.

"You've been asleep for about forty-five minutes," he said as he reached down to help me up.

"I was having a shitty dream," I said.

"Why shitty?" he asked.

"Well, I was in a…" I paused and thought.

"Never mind, it was stupid," I said.

"No, tell me. You'd be surprised what can be determined from someone's dreams," he said as he helped me to my feet.

There was a lot I would tell Erik, and very little I would ever keep from him, if anything. Something about telling a psychiatrist about my dreams, and that psychiatrist being my boyfriend didn't make me totally comfortable.

"Oh, it was nothing," I said.

"You sure?" he asked.

"Yeah, now that I am awake, I can't really remember it" I said.

"Well, I have a few lights left, even after I put them over the entire roof," he said.

I looked around the roof, and back toward Erik. I was still waking up. I felt like such an idiot for falling asleep.

"Baby girl, reach over there and put your hands on the roof. The one right in front of you, by the bedroom window," Erik said as he set the staple gun down beside me.

"Sir?"

"The roof, Kelli. Put your hands on it. Are you having problems with English again?" he asked.

"Uhhmm, no sir," I responded as I leaned forward and placed my palms on the roof. Standing erect directly in front of the window, the roof was about chest high.

"Don't move, I'll be right back," Erik said as he walked across the roof.

I stood with my hands on the roof above the window wondering

Baby Girl III

what he was going to do. I blinked my eyes and looked around. That dream was just weird. He walked back toward me with a handful of Christmas lights in his hand.

I watched over my shoulder as he took out his knife and cut the Christmas light cord in two. He put the knife back in his pocket and secured the clip.

"Why did you cut the Christmas lights?" I asked, confused.

"I need two, and I only had one," he responded, smiling.

I squinted and turned toward him.

"Hands on the fucking roof, Kelli. Face the window," he demanded, pointing at the window by the bedroom roof.

I turned and faced the window, and placed my hands on either side of the roof in front of my chest.

I watched his reflection in the window as he took the Christmas lights and flipped one of the two lengths over his shoulder. He dropped the other string of lights onto the roof, holding onto one of the ends of the cord. He raised the cord up to his chest and grabbed the dangling length with his other hand. He stepped into me, pressing his chest to my back.

"Raise your right hand," he said as he bent over and picked up the staple gun.

"Sir?" I asked as I turned toward him.

"Around Kelli, turn around. And raise your right hand. You remember which one that is?" he asked in his smart-ass voice.

I purposely raised my left hand. I love it when he talks to me like this. It makes me wet. I wondered what he was going to do. Maybe spank me with Christmas lights. I started to get wet thinking about it.

"Jesus, Kelli. I think that dream fucked you up good. Your other right hand. Good fucking God," he complained.

Get mad at me and hurt me. Fuck me until I cry.

I raised my right hand. The correct one.

He took my wrist in his hand and began to wrap my wrist in the chord of the lights. I watched as he wrapped my wrist in the lights and slipped the cord through itself and pulled it tight. He took the loose end in his hand and tugged on it.

"Put your hand back on the roof," he said.

I stared at my wrist as I put my hand back onto the roof. As my hand touched the shingles on the roof, he reached for the end of the Christmas light chord and pulled my arm tightly to the right.

BAM!

He began stapling the cord to the wooden shingles.

BAM…BAM…BAM!

BAM, BAM, BAM, BAM, BAM!

"That should do it. Pull against the chord," he said.

SCOTT

"You just stapled my hand to the roof," I said as I turned and looked at him over my shoulder.

"No, Kelli. I stapled the chord to the roof. Not your hand, the chord. Pull on it," he demanded as he smiled at me – obviously proud of his demented mind.

I pulled against the chord. It was no different than the night that he restrained and blindfolded me.

"Erik, we're on the roof," I said over my left shoulder.

"Damn, you have a good memory. Surprised you didn't forget after that nap you took," he said.

"Left hand, baby girl, raise it. This one is easy, it's the only one you have left," he laughed.

I raised my left hand. He bent over and picked up the remaining Christmas lights and doubled the chord over a few times, shaking the lights strand to make the lengths of cord even. He wrapped my hand in the chord, and slipped it through itself.

"Put it on the roof, baby girl," he said, smiling.

I reached to the left, shaking my head.

"What?" he asked.

"You enjoy this too much," I laughed.

"Shit, you've seen nothing yet, baby. You're stuck with me now, and eventually...every night, you have to fall asleep. Wait and see what I do to and with you," he laughed.

He pulled on the end of the cord until my arm was tight.

BAM...BAM!

He started stapling again.

BAM...BAM!

BAM, BAM, BAM, BAM, BAM!

"Pull against it," he demanded.

I pulled against the two cords.

Nothing.

I felt like Jesus crucified on the cross, my arms stretched out to my sides.

"Well, for the sake of fuck," he complained as he looked around the roof.

"What?" I asked as I looked over my shoulder.

"Well, I used all of my Christmas lights. I don't have anything for your legs. I can't tie your legs," he said in a very serious tone.

"Uhhmm, I can't go *anywhere*. A tornado couldn't blow me off of here," I said.

Our home was a few miles from the small airport outside of Benton. The airfield, originally, was used by local farmers. In recent years, from what Erik said, they refurbished it. People had built expensive homes along the taxiway, most of which had an aircraft hangar attached. The short length of the runway limited the size of aircraft that could land and take off, but there were always small aircraft flying in and out.

We were a few miles from the airport, and a few miles from the city limit of Wichita. Technically, we lived in the suburbs, but we didn't have any immediate neighbors. Our home did face the narrow two lane road that connected the airport to Wichita.

Erik reached in front of me and unbuttoned my jeans. He pulled them down to my ankles and removed my shoes. I watched as he set my shoes aside and folded my jeans and set them on top of the shoes. As he knelt behind me, he kissed my inner thighs.

He pressed his head between my legs and began to lick my pussy. As he licked, his finger slid in and out of my wetness. As he began to rub my clit with his fingertip, I felt my legs begin to shake.

Something about being tied to the roof was extremely exciting.

His finger slid in and out as he licked my pussy from the rear. I bent my knees and pressed my ass further into his face. He forced his tongue deeper and fingered me faster. I bit my bottom lip. His tongue fucked me deeper and faster. His finger tickled my clit. I bit my lip harder. And he began to moan as he licked me.

Oh God.

And.

I came.

I heard a vehicle, opened my eyes, and looked at the window. I watched as the reflection of a truck drove by. I wondered what anyone that drove by might think. I guess considering that Erik and I lived here, maybe people would get used to things like this.

He continued to suck my clit and lick my pussy. I wiggled, feeling sensitive from the orgasm.

I pulled on the cords.

I wasn't going anywhere. I swiveled my hips and felt my wet pussy against his face when I did.

"What the fuck are you doing?" he asked.

"Nothing," I laughed.

He stood up.

"Excuse me?" he said sharply as he put his hand on my neck.

Oh yes.

Please.

Squeeze it.

"Nothing sir," I responded as I stared at the shingles of the roof.

I heard his belt unbuckle. I looked down to my left as his pants hit the tops of his boots. I pulled on the cords again.

Shit.

"You want to escape me, baby girl?" he growled into my right ear.

"No sir," I squeaked.

I felt him penetrate my pussy with his stiff cock. His free hand reached around to my stomach and pulled my torso up and backward, forcing my ass to rise. I stood on my tip-toes. He began fucking me harder as he squeezed my neck with a little more force.

His hand on my neck was turning me on.

A trigger.

I pulled on the cords again.

"You're gonna get it, little girl," he growled.

He squeezed my neck harder.

He began to fuck me harder and shove himself deep. His hips pounding against my ass made slapping sounds with each stroke. Every inch of his cock was being forced into me. My calves ached from standing on my tip-toes.

I want him to squeeze my neck and fuck me hard.

Really hard.

I pulled on the cords again and growled. I shook my head from side-to-side.

Be careful of what you wish for. My father always told me that.

He squeezed my neck harder.

And pounded my pussy with force. His cock felt larger than it ever had.

He pulled against my neck, forcing my head closer to his face.

"You're not going to get away from me. You're stapled to the roof, you mouthy little shit," he whispered.

"Who owns you, you little slut?" he asked.

"You do," I squeaked. His hand was tighter on my neck than it had ever been.

But it wasn't tight enough.

"Who?" he growled into my ear. His hot breath almost made me cum.

Life offers us decisions. Sometimes we make good ones, and sometimes we make bad ones. When we make these decisions, we often take a chance, hoping that the outcome will be favorable. Making a split-second decision often produces results that we never expected. Turning back the clock and changing the clock and changing our mind is never an option. My father always told me to take three steps.

Think. Think. Act.

This was good advice.

With Erik, sometimes I just acted.

"Nobody. Fuck you, untie me!" I screamed as I pulled frantically on the chords.

He squeezed my neck harder. His fingers dug into my flesh and tightened around my neck. I felt him adjust his hand and grip again.

That's not tight enough, I want you to squeeze my neck, Erik.

"Let go of my neck, and untie me now. Nobody owns me," I screamed.

He squeezed even harder. He forced himself into my pussy like he was trying to kill me.

I began to contract with force.

His hips slapped against my ass.

I started to tingle from my head to my tip-toes.

This was going to be huge.

"If I don't own you now, I god damned sure will when we're done. You're mine, do you understand me?" he breathed into my ear.

I shook my head as best I could. I pulled against the chords and growled.

"Fuck you, untie me you cock sucker," I grunted.

That should do it.

His hand tightened around my neck and I felt him increase his intensity of forcing himself into my soaking pussy. I began to tingle from head to toe. My pussy felt like it was going to explode.

I yanked the cords.

He squeezed tighter and tighter.

I closed my eyes.

And my pussy exploded. I felt as if I was somewhere else. Certainly not on this earth. I opened my eyes. Everything got milky. I blinked my eyes. The lights were bright. I opened my eyes. Everything was gone.

Black.

I came. And came.

And came.

...

...

...

...

...

"Baby girl!" he barked.

I'm not sure if the time between the last time I opened my eyes and when I could finally see again was five seconds or five minutes. I have no way of knowing. All I know for certain is one thing.

One.

I'm figuring this out.

How to get what I want.

And keep Erik happy.

I fucking love this man with all that I am. With all that I can provide. I love him with my entire existence. He breathes life into me. He has allowed me to understand who I am, and not feel broken for being me. I can be myself with Erik and not worry about him criticizing me.

He owns me.

And he always will.

"Baby girl!" he said again.

I heard the click of his knife, and felt him cutting the cords.

I blinked my eyes, turned to face him and smiled.

"There's my baby girl," he said, smiling.

And he shuffled in front of me. With his pants around his ankles, on the roof of the house - the house that *we* owned - he kissed me deeply.

"I love you baby girl. I love you with all that I have, know that," he said softly as he held my face in his hands and looked into my eyes.

"I do," I said.

Every girl wants to say that to a man.

I do.

Chapter Eight

KELLI. "I don't know, Doc. Hell, there are a few options. A tread plate on the leading edge of the steps, carpeting them, and there's the sandpaper strips - but they will look like shit on these wooden steps," Bunny said.

"Well fuck, I don't know Bun, that's why *you're* here," Erik said as he looked up and down the stairs.

"Well, they're slick as snot, Doc. Hell, she'll fall half the time she comes down them if she comes in heels or socks," Bunny said.

I looked at Bunny and back at Erik. I always thought that Bunny was smaller than Erik, but he wasn't. They could be twins almost if Bunny didn't have a shaved head. Bunny was maybe an inch shorter than Erik, but you'd never know if they weren't side by side. Bunny wore jeans, Chuck's, and a white tee shirt. He had tattoos like Erik. One arm all the way to the wrist and one was tattooed to his elbow. I was studying his tattoos when Erik yelled at me.

"Are you paying attention, baby girl?" he asked.

"Uhhmm, not really. I didn't hear you," I answered.

Erik looked at Bunny with a puzzled look and back at me.

"We were talking to you, and you're standing there drooling. Wipe your lip, baby girl," he said.

Bunny laughed.

I wiped my mouth with the back of my hand. I had been slobbering. I felt like an idiot, I must have zoned out for a few minutes.

"Staring at you and slobbering. What do ya think of that, Bun?" Erik asked Bunny.

"Shit Doc, she was just in another world. Probably thinking about falling down these slick ass steps," he laughed.

"I was looking at his tattoos," I said.

SCOTT

"He's got more than me, huh Bun?" Erik asked as he stood up from his crouched position.

"Last I knew, I'd say so," he answered.

"Hell baby, Bunny even has 'em on his legs," Erik said, pointing to Bunny's legs.

"Oh, wow, I didn't know," I said, looking at his jeans, wondering what he had on his legs.

Erik walked to the utility room and left Bunny and I at the steps. He had his hand on his chin, and was looking up and down the steps.

"I guess it gets right down to what you prefer, Sis. You want carpet on them? I can match the carpet upstairs pretty good. The wood will stay here in the entry, but not on the steps," he said, pointing to the wooden floor we were standing on.

"Carpet sounds fun," I said.

"Fun?" he laughed and shook his head.

"Here we go, Bunny. Hell I can't believe you came and didn't bring a tape," Erik said, holding a tape measure in his hand.

"Well, I was just in the neighborhood. Shit Doc, I rode the bike," Bunny said apologetically.

"Guess I didn't realize you rode the sled. Here," Erik said as he handed him the tape measure.

"Go upstairs, Doc, hold it on the edge of the handrail," Bunny said as he extended the tape measure up toward the top of the stairs.

Erik went up the stairs and grabbed the end of the tape measure. Bunny pulled the other end to the floor.

"Alright," Bunny said.

"So where did you learn to do this?" I asked.

"My dad taught me, when I was a little kid," Bunny said.

"Oh, is it what he does?" I asked.

"Did. Yeah, it's what he *did*," he responded.

I stared at his tattoos. He twisted his arm around in a circle, showing me the rear of it. There was an anchor surrounded by a ribbon and a date with some initials. The date was 10 - 93.

"He was killed in Somalia. Probably about the time you were born," he said.

"I'm sorry," I said.

"Yeah, no changing it now, Sis," he responded.

I thought about Erik not having parents at all, and of Bunny not having a dad. I wondered how many of the guys that Erik rode with didn't have fathers, and if it was part of the reason that they rode in the club. Maybe not having a father made them want to be in the club for the camaraderie, and that union filled the void that their father left.

I was grateful that I had my father, and that he had always been there for me. Any time I needed him, he was always present. I imagined how hard it would be on me if my father had died, or if he wasn't in my life. Now that Erik and I were together, I imagined that Erik would feel a loss too - if my father was gone.

Erik came down the stairs and stepped between us.

"So, know what you need?" Erik asked.

"Yeah, if you know what you want," Bunny answered, laughing.

"Carpet?" Erik asked.

"Yes, I want carpet, it'll be fun," I responded

"Fun," they both said at the same time.

"Fun *to walk on*," I corrected myself.

"Carpet it is. When can you do it, Bun?" Erik asked.

"Well, I need to do it pretty quick. I am out of about all other side work, and I have to get as much done as I can, just to survive," he responded.

"Oh. Well hell. Let's get it done then, Bunny," Erik said as Bunny handed him the tape measure back.

"Sounds good, tell me when," he said.

"Okay. Well, this weekend. Next week, whatever," Erik said.

"I'll start tomorrow," Bunny said, "Be done by the end of the day."

"Damn, okay. How much?"

"Five hundred. That'll fix the porch handrail and get these stairs carpeted. I wouldn't charge you that much, but hell, Doc. You know, I've had a hell of a time finding work. I'm broke as fuck," he said.

"Deal, I'll have the cash here to pay you," Erik said.

"Sounds good. We'll get carpet on 'em. It'll be *fun*." Bunny laughed as he rubbed his head.

"Fun," I giggled.

Erik and Bunny both turned to me and laughed.

"I can't wait till you get carpet on them, then I can run up and down them as fast as I want," I said as I turned and smiled at Erik and then Bunny.

"Doc'll be right behind you, I suppose," Bunny laughed.

"Well, I better get. It was nice seeing you two. We'll get carpet on these tomorrow, and you two can do whatever you do, with no worries about getting hurt," Bunny said as he hugged Erik.

"Alright Bun," Erik said.

"Give me one, Sis," he said as he turned to hug me.

I've never had so many hugs in my life as I have had since I met Erik and the club. I liked it a lot.

"Gotta take care of my girl," Erik said.

"Take care of those that take care of us, Doc," Bunny said.

"Amen," Erik said.

Bunny walked to the door and opened it. He paused for a second. As he stepped through the door, it sounded like he spoke.

Amen.

Chapter Nine

*E*RIK. Loving Kelli was not a decision I consciously made. I had not in the past made a decision to do so, and I was not making one now. Loving Kelli was who I had become. My desire, contrary to what some may think, was to please her and make her proud to be by my side. The thought of ever having to be without her sickened me.

Any consideration of being without her for moments, hours, a day, or any amount of extended period of time was difficult at best. When she was away from me, I yearned for her to return. Kelli had, to me, become my reason to exist.

Entirely.

My idle moments were filled with thoughts that included her. I told her when we met that I wanted to witness her exist.

I like watching you walk. I like watching your mouth open and hearing the words form on your tongue. I want to know you. I don't want to know you from having you text me your favorite color, your favorite restaurant, and your list of favorite songs; I want to know you from exposure. I want to witness you exist. I want to absorb you.

The more I learned of who she was, the more grateful I was for her existence. This girl was, for me, perfect from the beginning.

Bam.

Bam.

Clunkety clunk.

Clunk.

"God damn it, baby girl, what are you doing?" I screamed as she came down the stairs, dragging behind her what appeared to be a bed sheet full of rocks.

She stopped half way down the stairs.

She stood there, on the newly installed carpet, naked.

"Uhhmm. Well. They're all dirty and covered in mud. I'm going to wash them, the pillowcases, and wash the sheets - they're covered in cum," she said, smiling as if she were at a photo shoot.

"*What*, Kelli? What's all muddy?" I asked as I stood up, walked toward, and approached the stairs.

"My Chuck's. All of them. I've been exploring out by the river. Did you know there's a river back there? And train tracks?" she asked from the middle of the rise of stairs.

"Yes, I knew. Jesus, it sounded like you were dragging a dead body down the steps," I laughed, now standing at the bottom of the steps.

"Nope, no dead body. Not unless you stop fucking me," she said as she started down the remaining steps.

Clunk.

Bam.

Clunkety clunk.

Bam.

"Excuse me," she said as she walked passed me, dragging the bed sheet full of pillow cases and shoes along the floor behind her naked body. As she walked passed, she bumped into me and turned toward the kitchen.

I watched her leg muscles flex as she walked through the kitchen. Her grace was amazing when she walked. It was as if she had been trained to do so. Watching her made me want to just...

Watch her.

"You know what I like about living here?" she screamed from the laundry room.

"What's that?" I asked as I walked into the kitchen.

"I like that I can just walk around naked. It's fun," she answered through the laundry room door.

"Oh, I didn't know you were coming in here, you scared me," she said as I leaned in the doorway.

She twisted the dial and pulled it out. The washing machine started running.

I reached over her shoulders and gripped her neck in my hand. As I pulled her close, I leaned toward her and kissed her lips lightly. I continued to kiss her lips and chin, eventually moving my way down to her neck.

As I kissed her neck, she moaned. With my left hand, I felt along the length of her back and onto her ass. I squeezed her butt cheek in my hands as I licked and kissed her collar bone.

She continued to moan as I kissed her. I pressed her against the washing machine and moved my way to her breasts, sucking them lightly and kissing her now swollen nipples. As I squeezed her breasts

Baby Girl III

with my left hand, I moved my mouth back to hers. Our lips touching lightly, I licked her upper lip with the tip of my tongue.

Squeezing her neck in my hand, we continued to kiss.

I closed my eyes and got lost in kissing her.

The washing machine clicked.

It started to shake as the cycle changed to *spin*.

As it began to gain speed, it started to vibrate aggressively.

And shake from side to side.

"It's not balanced, your load isn't balanced. What all did you put in there?" I asked as I looked up and toward the top of the machine.

"Chuck's" she said, standing between the machine and I.

"That's it?" I asked as I leaned forward and opened the lid of the machine.

"What in the fuck, baby girl? How many pairs are in there?" I asked.

The machine looked like a rainbow of canvas and white rubber soles.

"Eleven," she responded as she tried to pull the lid closed.

'They're not balanced," I said as I pushed the lid all the way open and released it from my grasp.

The machine began to slow down. I nudged my way beside her and looked inside at the mess of shoes.

She reached over the machine and slammed the lid closed.

The washer began to gain speed and shake violently. She placed her hands on the machine and boosted herself onto it. She wiggled into place and sat there shaking as the machine gained speed. Her breasts jiggled up and down as the machine rotated her eleven pair of unbalanced canvas sneakers.

I shook my head.

Any man on this earth that thought for one moment that Kelli wasn't absolutely the cutest woman on earth would be a damned fool. Her being submissive in no way, shape, or form made her weak. She was a strong woman, full of life, and was willing to take risks to get what she felt that she wanted. As she had become more comfortable with the fact that I wasn't going to leave her, she had opened up.

And I loved who she was.

My baby girl.

"That's it," I snarled in as angry of a tone as I could manage.

I reached in her direction.

"What?" she asked as she raised her eyebrows slowly.

"You're going to fuck up the machine. It's brand new. Get down," I demanded, trying to keep from smiling.

"No," she said, her breasts jiggling as the machine shook.

"Get down. Now," I demanded, my hands now on each side of her waist.

She shook her head from side to side, reached up slowly, and began to roll her nipples between her fingers and her thumbs.

I pursed my lips.

"Off, now," I scrunched my brow.

She shook her head and rolled her nipples in between her thumbs and index fingers. She closed her eyes and leaned her head back and shook it from side to side lightly and moaned. Her string straight black hair fell down onto the machine.

"That's it, you little fucker," I barked as I pulled her toward the front of the machine.

She opened her eyes and looked puzzled.

"Permission, Kelli. We're back to asking for permission, do you understand me?" I asked.

"Sir?" she questioned.

"Fucking permission. For orgasms. You're going to have to get permission to have one," I said as I placed a hand on the inside of each of her knees. I pressed her inner knees and spread her legs apart.

"Let go of your nipples and hold your legs apart, Kelli," I demanded.

"I can just hold them…" she said.

"Let go of your nipples, Kelli. Grab your knees and hold your legs apart. Do you understand me?" I asked in a low serious tone.

"Yes sir," she answered as she lowered her hands and cupped her knees in her palms.

"Do it, pull them apart for me," I said.

She spread her legs wider. As she did, her wet pussy glistened and opened slightly. She was clearly already very aroused.

"Do not move for any fucking reason, Kelli," I said as I turned to walk into the kitchen.

"Understand?" I asked over my shoulder as I walked through the door into the kitchen.

"Yes," she paused.

"Yes sir," she half stuttered, her breasts shaking as the washing machine shook.

I walked into the kitchen and opened the refrigerator. I opened the vegetable drawer and pulled out the sack with the jalapeno peppers in it. I reached into the sack and pulled out one of the peppers. I thought for a fraction of a second and gripped the pepper in my left hand. I squeezed the pepper in between my fingers and crushed it. I rubbed my fingers on the outside of the pepper for a second and tossed it into the sink.

I walked back into the laundry room and stopped in front of Kelli. Her breasts shook as the machine wiggled from side to side.

"Did you move?" I asked.

Baby Girl III

"No sir, you told me to sit here with my legs spread," she responded in a matter of fact tone.

'That's a good girl. And what do you do when I tell you to do something?" I asked.

"I do it," she responded.

"Yes, baby girl. Yes, you do," I stated.

"You don't want to disappoint me, do you?" I asked.

She shook her head side to side frantically.

"No sir, never," she said sharply.

"Ever?" I asked.

"No. Never," she said.

"Okay," I said as I knelt to the floor.

I positioned my head between her legs and licked her inner thigh. As my tongue worked toward her wet pussy, she moaned softly.

"You want me to lick your little pussy, baby girl?" I asked, looking up into her eyes.

She nodded repeatedly.

I moved my right hand to in between her legs. I pressed the palm of my left hand into the top of her right thigh. My tongue touched her pussy lips, she moaned loudly. I pulled my mouth from her pussy, and inserted my right index finger to the web of my hand.

"In and out, Kelli," I said.

"In and out. In and out," I repeated.

Each time I said *in*, I slid my finger all the way inside of her.

"In and out," I said as I licked her clit with the tip of my tongue and worked my finger in and out.

I squeezed her right thigh with my left hand.

"You like it when I lick your clit, baby?" I looked up and asked.

"Oh…oh God yes," she responded.

I leaned back and unzipped my pants. I unbuckled my belt and slid my pants to my feet. I kicked them beside the washer, which had since quit vibrating, and began filling with water. I reached up and turned the dial back to *spin*.

As the washing machine started to spin, it began to shake. Kelli began to moan. I reached down with my right hand and stroked my cock. Kelli leaned forward and stared as I stroked my cock.

"You like watching me stroke my cock, baby girl?" I asked.

"Uh huh…yes. Yes, sir," she said softly, never lifting her eyes from my cock.

"Jump down off of there, Kelli," I said.

She sprung to the floor immediately, and looked at me for instruction. She shifted her weight from foot to foot, obviously feeling aroused and anxious.

"You horny, baby girl?" I asked.

"Uh huh. Very. Uhhmm. *Yes, sir*," she said, nodding her head.

SCOTT

"Get down on your knees, baby. Suck my big cock, I want you to gag on it like a good girl," I said.

She immediately dropped to her knees and started licking the tip of my cock. She placed both her hands on her thighs and moved her mouth to meet the tip of my cock. She took half of it in her mouth, pressing the head to the roof of her mouth with her tongue. She slipped her mouth back along the shaft, and released my cock from her lips. As it fell from her mouth she moaned, licked her lips, and looked up into my eyes.

"I love sucking your cock," she said as she looked up into my eyes.

She wiggled her legs back and forth, her hands positioned between her knee and her lower thigh. Her mouth open wide, she moved it to meet the tip of my cock. She growled and pressed her mouth hard against the shaft, taking it all the way down her throat. As the tip worked its way into her throat, her throat convulsed. She held it there, groaning and moaning. She batted her eyelashes, my cock still deep in her throat.

She raised her hands slowly from her knees, and grasped my ass in her hands, my cock still deep in her throat. As she squeezed my ass, she pressed herself harder against the shaft. Her bottom lip touched my ball as she extended her tongue.

"Okay, that's it, stand up," I demanded as I pulled my cock from her throat.

She smiled and coughed as my cock cleared her lips. She slowly stood in front of me. As she wiped her mouth on the back of her hand, I placed my hands on her shoulders.

"Turn around, baby girl," I said as I pushed her shoulder toward the washing machine, rotating her body to face the machine.

"Put your hands on top of the machine and do not move them. Understand?" I asked.

She nodded her head.

"Do you understand me?"

"Yes sir," she responded.

"That's better. Turn the dial to rinse. Put your big titties on the machine," I demanded as I pushed on her back, forcing her to bend at the waist.

She bent down, turned the dial, and pressed her breasts to the machines surface. The machine quickly began to wobble. Using my foot, I spread her legs apart wider than her chosen stance. I gripped my cock in my right hand and stroked the shaft.

I guided my cock into her pussy and slowly pressed it into her all the way. As it slid inside, she moaned loudly.

"If you cum, I will slap the shit out of you," I barked.

She shook her head side to side.

"No sir. Sorry. No sir," she said apologetically.

I gathered her hair in my right hand and worked my way to the base of her skull. Gripping her hair tightly, I began to fuck her deep and slow.

"Count, Kelli, count the strokes. Every one of them," I said.

"Sir?" she asked.

"Count God damn it. You can still count, right? Seventy-seven. I know you can count that high. Count my fucking strokes," I said in a stern tone.

"Yes sir," she said.

I pulled her hair, arching her back and slid my cock inside of her until my hips are against her ass. I held it there. She said nothing. I pulled her hair sharply.

"Oh, uhhmm. One," she said.

I slid my cock back slowly and pressed it back inside until my hips pressed her round ass.

"Two."

I repeated the stroke.

"Three."

I slowly slid my cock all the way out of her wet pussy and stepped back, admiring her ass and pussy. I moved closer to her and guided my cock back inside of her. Slowly, I slid it inside.

"Four."

I held it in place and took a deep breath. She moaned.

"Don't you dare," I said.

And I began to fuck her as hard and as fast as I could.

"Five. Six. Seven. Eight. Nine, Ten. Ten. Eleven. Oh fuck. Thirteen."

"Please?" she asked.

"No. Not yet," I responded.

She bent her knees and straightened them back to standing. My cock slammed in and out of her soaking wet pussy. It sounded like I was slapping her ass with my hands.

"Oh, God Erik. Uhhmm. Fifteen. Oh. Fuck."

"Now? Can I cum?"

"No."

I pulled her hair. She arched her back more. The washing machine wobbled furiously.

"Press your fucking titties to the washer and count, damn it," I growled through clenched teeth.

"Seventeen. Eighteen. Oh God. God. I'm going…I'm gonna…"

"You better not say cum," I reminded her in a stern tone.

I slowed my pace of fucking her.

"Twenty. Twenty-one….oh fuck. Oh fuck," she squealed.

She bent and straightened her knees.

"Now? Can I…"

SCOTT

"Goddamnit, No!"

I slid my cock from inside her pussy. Using my left hand, I reached down and wiped my index finger against her pussy. It was soaking wet. I took my now wet finger and slid it up the crack of her ass. As I guided my cock back into her pussy, I slowly slid my left index finger into her ass.

Slowly, I slid my finger in and out of her ass. She began to moan. I then slid my cock deep inside of her. And I held it there.

"Count," I demanded.

"Uhhmm. Oh. Twenty-five. Yeah, twenty-five," she said.

I began to slowly work my cock and finger in and out of her pussy and ass at the same time. As I did, she counted.

"Twenty-six, twenty-seven, twenty-eight, twenty-nine, thirty, thirty-one," she bit her lower lip and mumbled as she spoke.

"Oh God, uhhmm. Now?" she begged.

"No, that's it. Don't ask again."

"Sir?"

"You heard me," I responded.

I continued to fuck her slowly.

"Oh God. Oh…my..Uhhmm. Oh my. Uhhmm. Thirty-two. Oh God," she shook her head.

"Hot. Hot. Uhhmm, thirty. Hot…it's hot," she started to turn around.

"Tits on the washer, and count," I demanded as I pulled her hair harder.

"Oh. Uhhmm, Oh fuck. God. Uhhmm thirty something, Oh God," she mumbled as I sped up my pace.

"Fuck it Kelli, cum. Cum. Just fucking cum," I shouted as I began to fuck her faster.

I pounded my cock in and out of her pussy. My finger worked in and out of her ass as I fucked her. As I fucked her ass and wet pussy, I tightened my strain on her hair.

"Oh God…Oh God Erik," she squeaked.

I fucked her harder.

The washing machine wobbled.

I pulled her hair, forcing myself deeper into her as I did. I felt my cock begin to swell. I wasn't going to last much longer.

"Oh god. I'm going to…" she squeaked.

"Do it," I demanded.

I worked my cock and finger in and out of her pussy and ass. She bent and straightened her legs a few times and stood up straight, locking her knees.

My breathing quickened. My cock felt as if it were going to explode. I pushed my finger into her ass deep.

As I erupted inside of her, she screamed and bent her knees. I slowly slid my finger out of her ass. And pressed my cock deep, feeling the surge of cum discharge inside of her. I moaned.

"Oh my fucking..." she cried.

Her legs bent and straightened twice.

The washing machine stopped wobbling.

"God."

Her entire body shook. I released her hair and leaned my upper body back, admiring her physique. I kept my cock buried deep inside of her.

She moaned and shook. Her legs quivered one last time. She bent her knees and straightened them again. I pulled my cock slowly from her pussy. As it did, I could see that we were both covered in her cum. She shook her head, and turned to look at me.

"What the fuck?" she asked.

I smiled.

"I think I squirted again," she said.

"Good, how'd it feel," I asked.

"Don't talk to me," she said as she lowered her head onto the washing machine.

"You alright?" I asked.

"No. Not even close," she said, her face pressed into the lid of the washing machine.

"My ass is on fire, I just had an orgasm like nothing I have ever felt, I'm covered in cum, and you're trying to make me talk to you. No I am not alright," she said as she wobbled her head from side to side - her forehead resting on the surface of the machine.

"Yeah but I think your shoes are clean," I laughed as I slapped her on the ass.

God I love this woman.

Chapter Ten

*E*RIK. To me, in life, there has always been what we think and what we feel. The two are separated by *feeling*. The non-thinking. The happening. Thinking requires thought processes, planning, decisions, and implementation. Feeling never has come easy for me, but when it happens, there's not a thing you can do to stop it.

If you have to think about love, it isn't true and it isn't love. If love happens into your life, if love is something that you one day magically *feel*, it's real, true, and forever.

Go with what you feel.

Leave the thinking for mathematics and matters of finances. Thinking is not meant to be utilized when it comes to love. Love just happens. *Love just is*. Love consumes us and provides us with the ability to conquer whatever we encounter that gets between us and who we love.

Love makes us strong. Love builds walls. Walls that protect us from the outside forces that attempt to sabotage it. True love is self-sufficient and can survive any series of traumatic events, because love isn't a mere thought, it consumes us.

Go with what you feel.

Kelly caused me to feel. I didn't think. I woke up feeling love for Kelli. I fell asleep feeling it. If I was breathing, I was full of love for Kelli.

Erik Ead in love.

Sounds like a fucking oxymoron. My mother sure would be proud.

I reached into the console and turned off the slip control of the BMW. With the control off, there was nothing to prevent the tires from spinning. I looked ahead to make sure the intersection was free of traffic.

Free it was.

I downshifted twice and pushed the accelerator to the floor. I took the corner deep, sliding sideways through the intersection. The car accelerated through the corner, gaining speed as it slid. A glace in the rearview mirror provided a glimpse of the smoke from the rear tires. I shifted into second, and the car continued to spin and slide. As It gained traction, I shifted again, quickly accelerating up the street. I glanced at the speedometer.

122 miles per hour.

Not bad for a 30 mile per hour zone. I let off the accelerator and shifted the car to neutral.

I saw the lights before I heard the siren.

I steered the car into an abandoned grocery store lot and parked. The officer pulled in behind me and turned off his siren, leaving his lights flashing. I pulled my driver's license and held it in my left hand. I rolled my driver's side window down and looked through the window as I shut off the ignition.

This was going to hurt.

"Doc?" the officer said as he approached the car.

I looked over my shoulder and up at the officer. As I did, he removed his glasses and shook his head.

"God damn, Doc. Where's the fire? Jesus. I think I got you on the deceleration, and it was 131. That's jail time. What in the fuck were you thinking?" he asked.

"Snake? How's that new Road King running?" I asked, referencing his newly purchased motorcycle.

"Don't turn this into a biker romance thing, Doc. You could have killed someone," he looked over my car from front to rear.

Snake was an officer in the police department, and had been so for about ten years. He never moved up the ranks from being a beat cop because every time he turned around he was involved in some form of questionable practices. He never got into trouble, per se, but he was always close.

He rode with the local chapter of the police officer's motorcycle club. We were all friendly to one another, and although our club wasn't particularly friendly with the police officers, they were always friendly to us. Most of them.

"What the fuck is this thing? Some kinda race car?" he asked as he raised one eyebrow.

"It's an M3, Snake. Yeah, for the most part. Hell, I never drive like that," I apologized.

Snake turned and looked around the parking lot. He placed his hands on each side of his hips and exhaled a slow breath as he shook his head.

"One hundred miles an hour over the speed limit, that's not something that just happens, Doc," he said, still shaking his head.

"Oh, don't get me wrong, I *meant* to do it. It was planned. It's just not *common*," I said, still holding my license in my hand.

"Give me a good reason for you doing that. One," he said, both eyebrows now raised and focused on me.

I set the license on the console of the car, opened the door and got out. He stepped away from the door, making a little distance between he and I.

I stood and looked him in the eye intently.

"There's one and one only, and I truly apologize. But Snake, I am in love. Madly," I said, smiling from ear to ear.

"You? Give me something else, I know better," he said.

"I'm serious," I said, still smiling.

"Doc, you're a whore. You're in love with the entire female population," he laughed.

"Not any more. I'm in love with Kelli Parks," I said.

As I spoke, I shuffled my feet into a tap dance that would have rivaled anything ever produced by Sammy Davis, Jr. or Dean Martin.

He took a few steps back and watched my feet.

I stopped dancing and smiled.

"You're serious?" he said.

I nodded.

"Son-of-a-bitch, Doc," he exhaled and looked around the empty lot. He walked to his car and turned off the lights.

He opened the door and began talking into the radio microphone. He placed the microphone back into the center of the car, and shut the door.

"Being in love isn't a reason to be a damned fool. Remember that. Hell, I've been married three times," he said.

"Duly noted," I said.

"So, where's this leave us?" I asked.

"Tell you what. I'm gonna let you go. Next time I see you with a woman, I'm going to ask her what her name is. If she says it's Kelli, fine. If it's anything but that, I'm going to write you a ticket for 131 miles an hour. You'll lose your license for a few years. How's that?" he asked.

"I'm sorry, Snake," I said.

"Aww hell. Just get out of here. What are you doing out so early anyway?" he asked.

As I opened the car door I turned and raised one eyebrow.

"I don't want to know, never mind," he said as he opened his door and got into the car.

As I pulled from the parking lot, I thought of the serious nature of my driving at such a speed in town. It was ridiculous. It was dangerous. It was illegal.

It was fun.

Slowly, I drove up the street to Steve Wallace's place. I pulled into the lot and parked. Pat met me at the door, holding it open.

"How's it going, Wally?" I asked.

"Shit, Erik. One day at a fucking time," he responded as he let go of the door, making room for me to walk in.

"So, you bring the money?" he asked.

"Are you fucking serious?" I asked as I stopped and stared at him, my brow furrowed.

"Just asking, deals like this make me nervous," he responded.

"Let's see it," I said.

He placed a large wooden box about six inches deep and the size of a magazine on the table in front of him. I opened the box and looked inside.

"This is it?" I asked as I looked up from the box and into his eyes.

He nodded.

"Fuck yes," I muttered.

"One forty?" I asked.

"One forty-six, and not a penny less. You tight fisted prick. You're always wanting a deal. You got one hundred forty six grand in that pocket of yours?"

"Nope, got it in the car. I like round numbers, you sure one forty won't get it done?"

"Quite," he said as he slammed the lid closed.

"Don't get all pissy, Wally. Be back in a second," I said as I turned toward the door.

I pushed the button on the key fob releasing the trunk. I reached in and grabbed a small metal case intended to be used to transport handguns. I turned, stepped back to the door, and walked inside.

"*What the fuck*, Erik?" Wally asked as I walked inside, staring at the case.

"Oh, shit. No. It's *money*. The money's in here," I said apologetically.

"Sorry, brother, I wasn't thinking," I continued.

"That shit makes me nervous," he sighed.

I opened the box and handed it to him. Wally had been in a gunfight with some gang members a few years back, and was shot several times in the chest. It took about a year in the hospital for him to recover to the point that he could get back to work. A good portion of it he was in a coma. Guns made him extremely nervous now.

"Count it?" I asked.

"Nope, you're solid," he said.

"Come back in a week," he said as he carried the case to the back of the room.

I nodded, turned to the door and paused.

A week.

A week is a long time.

For some people.

It's all perspective.

Chapter Eleven

*K*ELLI. "It seemed for a while like we were growing apart. You know, as friends," she said.

"I felt the same way," I agreed.

"Well, it doesn't feel like that anymore," Heather said.

"Nope," I smiled as I shook my head from side to side.

"I think I was jealous for a while. You and Teddy were making progress and Erik and I weren't," I admitted.

"Well, you're all caught up *now*," she said, waving her hand around, motioning to the room.

"I know. Oh my God, this shit is insane," I said.

"Which one is it?" she asked.

"That one with that crazy bitch in it. *Christy Cross*. It's so fucking funny, but I'm afraid I can't finish it. It's way too hot. I want Erik to fuck me so bad, and he's gone till tonight," I laughed as I crossed my legs and rolled over onto my stomach.

"You bed pig, move over," Heather said as I got close to her.

"I'm reading *Kendall Grey, Strings*. Holy shit, that little bitch is crazy," Heather said.

"Which one," I laughed.

"Both. Oh my God, have you seen her status updates?" she asked.

"Kendall's? No," I responded.

"She gets so mad. She's funny. I can't fucking wait 'till *Nocturnes* comes out," she said.

"She hasn't friended me, I asked twice," I said.

Heather smiled. To Heather, having a friend like Kendall Grey was an accomplishment. I suppose all things considered, it was. I didn't look at Facebook as anything but a way for me to look at the book blogs and receive book recommendations. I used my Kindle to have a way to escape reality. Since Erik and I were actively together, I was spending much less time reading.

"I got this *Christy Cross* book from *Dirty Hoes* blog, I won a contest," I said.

"*Dirty Hoes*? Do you ever see *Snarky Bloggers* reviews?" Heather asked.

"You like her because her name's Heather," I laughed.

"No, I like her because she's fucking funny," she said.

"*Word Wenches* is the shit. They make awesome recommendations. And, uhhmm...*Book Bobbin*," I said as I turned the page.

"Babblin'. You dork. It's *Book Babblin'*. Bobbin. You little weirdo," she laughed.

"Whatever. *Brit Nanny*, That *Miria Vanessa* from *Life Between Fiction*, *Kathi White*, and *Cara Ross* all said this book was good. And it is; it's just *too much*. That scene with that guy deep throating that other guy. I about died," I laughed.

"Spoiler alert," she laughed as she rolled over onto her back, looking up at her Kindle.

"Oh my God, you still have that shirt?" I asked as she rolled over.

She smiled and rubbed her hands on her boobs. She was wearing her number eleven tee shirt from high school volleyball. She looked at it as good luck.

"Yes, I still have this shirt, and don't spoil the book, you tramp," she said as she stared at her Kindle.

"Whatever, you already knew it. They were talking about it in that thread the other day. Remember, the guy blew cum all over his face then shoved his cock back down his throat while she was sucking off the guy and poking a dildo up his ass," I said as I crossed my legs again.

"Oh. Fuck, yeah, I remember. Yeah, that book is insane from what they said. Gross," she said as she rolled back to her stomach.

"It's not gross, it's hot," I said.

"Different strokes," she said, looking up from her Kindle.

Reading had always been a way for me to escape everything. I felt when I read, if the writing was good enough, that I was the character in the book. It was nice to find someone that wrote in a manner that would pull me into the book and make me forget for a few hours who I was and where I was in my life.

Kendall Grey was one of those people. She made me, even though her books were insanely funny, feel like I was elsewhere. She made me laugh, cry tears of hilarity, and play with myself. I rubbed my clit a few hundred times to Kendall's books. Right now, I wanted to be rubbing it to *Christy Cross*.

"I'm going to the bathroom," I said as I slid off the edge of the bed.

Baby Girl III

"Leave your Kindle here," Heather laughed.

"Uhhmm, no," I giggled, clutching it to my chest.

"You're sick," she said, never raising her head up from her Kindle.

"It's why Erik loves me, I'm sick," I said.

I walked toward the master bathroom. Our new house was so nice. Having a bathroom in my bedroom was something I continually wanted as a kid. I had one down the hallway growing up, but had dreamed of having one in my *own bedroom*. Living here with Erik was beyond what my wildest dreams could ever conjure up.

"Teddy loves me because I'm beautiful," she said as I stepped into the bathroom.

"That and because you have huge tits," I snapped over my shoulder.

I stepped into the bathroom and shut the door.

I pulled down my pajamas and sat down. I flipped through the pages of the Kindle until I found a sex scene. As I read, I relaxed and relieved myself. I wiped and situated myself into the seat. As I read the scene, I paused, and looked up at the picture on the wall.

I couldn't do it.

Masturbation had lost all excitement.

I stood up and flushed the toilet.

He was right.

I was ruined.

Chapter Twelve

KELLI. "I want the chai latte. No, dirty chai," I said as I looked up at the menu.

"Regular, Erik?" Warren asked.

Erik nodded as he reached for his money.

"Let me pay for this," I said.

"Okay," he said as he waved his arm toward the counter.

"It's not very often a pretty girl will pay for your drink," Warren laughed as he prepared the drinks.

"True," Erik said as he walked to the table and sat down.

Ann handed me my card back and smiled, "Thanks, Kelli."

I smiled and walked to the table. I felt as if this was our place. We met here for the first time. Although we had technically *met* before, this was the first place that we met away from my work. This was our first date. I looked up at the disco ball and smiled.

"I love this place," I said as I sat down.

"Best coffee in town," Erik smiled as Warren handed him his coffee.

"Yours will be right up Kelli," he smiled.

I smiled back, "Thank you Warren."

"I kind of feel like this place is special. This was our first date," Erik said.

"I was just thinking that exact same thing. That's so weird," I said.

"What's weird?" he asked.

"That I was thinking the same thing," I responded.

"What's weird about it? It's true, this *was* our first date," he said as he took a sip from the cup.

"Here you go Kelli," Warren said as he handed me my coffee.

"I love the chai here. It's like Christmas in a cup," I said.

"You like Christmas, baby girl?" Erik asked.

I took a drink and nodded, "Yes, I love it."

"I used to, maybe I will again now. The lights will help a lot. Haven't had Christmas lights since," he looked up at the disco ball.

"Shit, I don't know. Well, it's been. I don't know. Maybe fifteen years, maybe more," he said as he focused back on me.

"Wow, I don't know what to say. We have our own now. That's what matters," I said as I took another drink.

"That's right," he said as he leaned over the table.

He placed his right hand on the back of my neck and pulled my head close to the middle of the table and leaned toward me. As his face got close to mine, he moved my hair beside my ear with his other hand. *When he does this it makes me melt.* His warm breath in my ear made me shiver.

"Baby girl," he whispered.

"Yes," I whispered back.

"I fucking love you," he whispered. His warm breath sent chills down my spine.

"I fucking love you back," I said.

"Baby girl," he whispered.

Baby Girl. That did it, I'm waaaaay wet.

"Yes," I whispered in a barely audible tone as I squirmed in my seat.

"I'm going to shove you so full of cock when we get home that you will not be able to walk tomorrow. We're going to have to get you a wheel chair. Do you understand me?" he asked as he squeezed the back of my neck with his hand.

I shifted in my seat. My pussy was a mess. I thought of Erik's cock inside of me. I liked watching it slide in and out of my pussy. When I watched it, it made me cum quickly. Erik's cock was like a chunk of velvet flesh. Hard velvet. Hard soft velvet. Hard and soft at the same time. Sometimes when he fucked me...

"I asked you a question," he forced his breath into my ear a little harder to get my attention.

"Oh, I was daydreaming," I whispered back.

"Ask Warren if he has a wheelchair you can borrow," he whispered.

"Sir?" I asked, turning my head to see his facial expression.

"I told you to ask Warren if he had any wheelchairs. You're going to need one," he laughed as he whispered in my ear.

"Warren?" I asked across the coffee shop.

"What do you need, Kelli?" Warren asked.

"Do you have any wheelchairs?" I responded.

"Do I what?" he asked back as he walked toward the table.

"Have a wheelchair?" I asked as he placed his hands on our table.

"No. No, Kelli, I don't have one. I don't know that I need one. Why?" he asked.

"Well, rumor has it I'm going to *need* one tomorrow. I thought maybe you may have one to borrow," I said, turning to smile at Erik.

"Oh yeah? Well, maybe the medical supply on Hillside. They rent them. Up by the hospital," he said as he shook his head and laughed.

"Yuck, I hate hospitals. They creep me out. People die in them," I said as I shook my head.

"There, satisfied?" I asked as I turned my head toward Erik.

He squeezed my neck in his hand, and pulled my face close to his.

"Full. Of. Cock. Do you understand me?" he whispered loudly in my ear.

"Yes sir. Full," I whispered back.

"Who fucking owns your sexy little ass?" he asked.

Wetness.

"You do," I responded.

He released my neck and sat back in his chair. I took a drink of my chai. As I tipped the cup up, something shuffled in the cup. I shook it. Something rattled. I looked at Erik. He shrugged as I pulled the lid from the cup.

Two quarters were in the bottom of the cup.

I turned the cup so Erik could see into the bottom.

"Shit, baby girl, you're rich," he said.

"Warren, why is there money in the bottom of my cup?" I asked across the coffee shop.

Warren laughed so hard he had tears in his eyes. He put his hands on his knees and giggled. I looked at Ann. She walked into the storage room and laughed. I looked back at Erik.

He shrugged.

"It wasn't *that* funny," I said.

"One is from Ann, and one is from me, they're your house warming gifts, Kelli. It wouldn't have been a gift if it wasn't wrapped. Ann and I weren't able to come to your party, so we thought we'd give you those. Times are tough, and we have a head down on the machine. Might cost ten grand to fix it," he said, still laughing.

"Oh, okay. Do you have an envelope? I don't want to get them mixed up with the others," I said.

Ann walked into the back room and got an envelope. She walked back out to the table and handed it to me and smiled.

"There you go, Kelli," she said.

I nodded and smiled, "Thank you."

I dumped the quarters onto the table and wiped them off with a napkin. I placed them into the envelope and got a pen from my purse and marked it.

House warming gifts from Espresso A Go Go, 2013.

I folded the envelope and placed it in my purse with the pen. I looked up at Erik and smiled as I placed my purse back in the window ledge.

"*Our* house warming gifts," I said.

"For *our* house," Erik responded.

"Ours. And our special coffee shop," I said.

"Ours," he responded.

I love hearing him say that.

Ours.

Chapter Thirteen

KELLI. "Why?" he asked me.
"Because I feel...I don't know. It's hard to explain," I said.

"Do your best," he said.

I thought about what he asked me. It wasn't easy to explain. It wasn't easy for me to even understand. It was just easy to *do*, especially with Erik. I liked that he made all of the decisions, for the most part. I enjoyed the thought of him owning me, and of this relationship slowly developing onto the one that it would one day become.

"I think it's just because for the first time in my life I haven't had to think. I think that may be one of them. Probably a big one," I said.

"I'm sure that's *part* of it," he said as he crossed his legs.

I sat and looked at the floor. I stared at the carpet until my vision blurred. I couldn't find words to describe it. *It just was.*

I looked up and shrugged my shoulders.

"Who owns you?" he asked from the couch he was sitting on.

"You sir," I responded.

"You're a good girl for me, aren't you baby girl?" he asked.

I nodded repeatedly, "Yes sir, I am."

"You ever going to disappoint me, baby girl?" he asked.

I shook my head from side to side. I hated when he even asked me this. I would never disappoint Erik. The thought of it made me sick to my stomach.

"No, never," I responded.

"Because you're my baby girl, and you're going to do what I ask of you," he said as he nodded his head slowly.

I nodded.

"Yes sir," I said.

"Can I come over there now," I asked, pointing to the couch.

He shook his head side to side.

"No," he responded.

I wanted to go sit beside him. He told me I had to sit in the chair and we were going to talk. I didn't like this. I wanted to be beside him. Touching him. Smelling him. Having him touch me. I have been good, and I have not done anything stupid in a long, long time. He should let me sit by him.

"I want to…"

"Kelli," he said sternly.

I looked down at the floor.

"How does it make you feel when I put my hand on the back of your neck and grip it with my hand, baby girl? While we're talking or standing in the kitchen?" he asked.

I nodded, "I love it."

"How does it make you *feel*?" he asked.

I thought for a second before I answered.

"Comfortable. Sleepy. Relaxed."

He nodded slowly, his hand still on his chin.

"When I tell you I am proud of you?" he asked.

"Happy. Like I'm doing a good job of being a good girl for you. Kind of like I have accomplished something," I said.

"When I tell you you're a good girl?" he asked.

"It's kind of the same - but just not as much. Like being a good girl and you being proud are kind of the same. You being proud, it's just better. It kind of means more," I said.

He nodded again and rubbed his face with his hand.

"When I squeeze your neck while we're fucking, how about that?" he asked.

I closed my eyes.

I love it when he does that.

"I love it. *I love it*. On the roof, I loved it so much. I think I passed out. It was. Well, I don't know how to explain it, but I love it," I said as I opened my eyes.

"Well, you didn't pass out, but I understand. It's euphoric, Kelli. It certainly isn't for everyone, but it can be very euphoric."

"Put it on the list of what I really, *really* like," I said.

"When I slap your little ass?"

"Love it," I said.

"Restrain you?" he asked.

I thought about what he asked.

"Tie me up?" I asked.

He nodded, "Yes."

"Love it," I said.

"Blindfolded," he asked.

I thought. I made a face and started to answer.

"Be truthful, Kelli. We're just talking. I need to know," he said, sitting up on the couch cushion.

"I don't think I like it," I said, making a face again.

"Okay. What about when I call you a little slut. *My little slut.* While were fucking?" he asked.

I nodded my head repeatedly.

"Love it," I said.

This was making me wet. All of this talking. As long as he didn't talk about me disappointing him, I liked it. All of this talk about sex, and being his slut, and baby girl...it was making me soaking wet. I wanted him to fuck me.

"Watermelon," I said.

"Excuse me?" he asked.

"Penelope," I said.

He smiled.

"Perpendicular" I said.

"You have a good memory," he said smiling.

I sat up on the edge of my cushion.

"Come here, baby girl," he said.

I bounced off the cushion of the chair and ran across the living room floor to the couch. I sat beside him and wrapped my arms around him.

"How'd I do?" I asked.

"Kelli, it wasn't a pass or fail. We were just talking. We're still learning about each other. Finding out what works and what doesn't. I'm not someone that ever wants to do anything to hurt you. I've told you that. I don't want to hurt you emotionally or physically. If we don't communicate, it's just guesswork. I hate guessing," he said.

"Communication is key," I said, nodding my head sharply at the end.

"Precisely," he said.

I kissed his cheek.

"We're going to play a game. A numbers game," he said, turning his head my direction.

"I love games," I said.

"Get on your knees in front of me, baby girl," he said.

Yaaaaaaay.

I got in front of him and looked into his eyes. He was going to let me suck his cock. I loved sucking his cock. He always let me fuck him after I sucked his cock. I loved sucking it anyway, but he could never take it for too long. He stood from the couch and pulled down his sweats. He kicked them to the side and pulled his tee shirt over his head. He grabbed his cock in his hand and slowly started stroking it, talking while he did.

"Okay, listen good,"
I watched him stroke his cock.
"Look at me, and pay attention, Kelli," he said.
I looked up into his eyes.

"I'm going to *tell* you to do things, additionally I'm going to do things *to* you. You're not going to tell me when you're going to cum. You're not going to tell me while you're cumming. When I ask, you're going to give me a number, between one and ten, describing how much you like or are enjoying what is happening - or what I am doing. This will be based on your level of enjoyment, euphoria, or how you feel. Ten is the most or best, one is the least or worst. You are not allowed to talk, unless it's a number. Do you understand?" he asked.

I nodded.
"Are you certain?" he asked.
I nodded.
"Baby girl, suck my big cock," he said.
"Ten!" I screamed as I clapped my hands.
"No, Kelli. You haven't experienced any *feeling* yet," he laughed.
"I want to know how you feel, based on exactly what's happening, okay?" he asked, looking down at me.
I nodded.
"Put my cock in your mouth," he demanded.

I grabbed his ass in my hands and squeezed it. I loved having his ass in my hands. I felt like he was mine when I did. It was like for a little while, I owned *him*. I opened my mouth and guided it onto his cock. As I squeezed his ass, I slowly began slurping on his cock, making it wet. Slowly, I began to suck it and think of how I felt.

I liked sucking Erik's cock, because I knew he liked it when I did it. Sucking his cock, I never wondered if he enjoyed what I offered him. I liked it too, because I felt like I was in total control. It wasn't *him* fucking me; it was *me* sucking his cock. If I was doing a good job, the reward was having him cum. When he said he couldn't stand it any longer, I knew I was doing a good job and making him happy. When he moaned and closed his eyes, it was a huge turn on.

I began to take more of him in my mouth. He arched his back and pressed his hips forward. As he did, his cock went deep into my throat. My throat convulsed and I swallowed. This process of my throat convulsing and me swallowing was similar to a feeling of vomiting, but different. It was a huge turn on for me, and it wasn't unpleasant. It was my way of gagging on his cock. I don't know why, but I loved it.

He held his cock deep in my throat until my eyes watered. I squeezed his ass hard in my hands, my fingers digging into the flesh. I wanted to pull my mouth off, but he didn't want me to. I closed my

Baby Girl III

eyes and hoped for him to pull away. As I felt his cock slipping from my throat, I opened my eyes and looked up at his face. I felt the wetness of my pussy as I shifted my weight on my knees. I was soaked.

He held his hands up and raised his eyebrows as his cock fell from my mouth.

I gasped for a breath and wiped my mouth.

"Uhhmm," I caught my breath, "Ten. Big ten."

"Hands and knees Kelli." he demanded.

I moved to my hands and knees. He got behind me and grabbed my waist. As he grabbed my waist, his cock slowly slid inside of my soaked pussy. Slowly, he began to slide in and out, pressing deep and slow. The rhythm of him fucking me caused my pussy to contract quickly. I closed my eyes and began to cum.

As my eyes began to roll I thought about the feeling and what it would be rated. I loved cumming, and I loved his cock, but I didn't want to rate it too high, because he could be doing so many other things. Good things.

His cock slowly and predictably slid in and out. I began to cum again.

"Six," I muttered.

He gathered my hair in his hand. He started to pull it lightly. I said nothing. He began to fuck me harder, his balls banging against my clit. I closed my eyes and listened to the sound of his hips against my ass. I loved that slapping sound. As his cock worked in and out of my soaked pussy, I felt myself tingle from head to toe. I remained quiet.

Nothing changed.

He didn't say I couldn't moan.

"Mmmmmmm," I moaned.

He pulled my hair harder, forcing himself deeper.

"Mmmmmmm," I moaned again.

He pulled my hair harder. I arched my neck back. The feeling of having my neck pulled backward was exciting to me. It was like being choked. Once I let my head go backward, it was impossible for me to pull it forward again – against his grasp on my hair. It was second best to being choked. I shook my head and tilted it back as far as I could. He pulled all the slack as I moved. My throat felt constricted.

I groaned.

"Ohhhhhhh," I groaned slowly.

Whack!

He slapped my ass hard with his free hand.

I waited a second.

"Mmmmmmm,' I moaned.

Whack!

"Mmmmmmm."

Whack!

Whack!

He pulled my hair harder. My eyes watered. I could barely breathe. He began fucking me harder, moving my knees across the floor. I moved my hands wider and tried to hold myself still. I felt as if his cock was in my throat. I contracted and felt as if I were going to explode. The feeling of tingling started in my throat and worked its way to my pussy and exploded.

I opened my eyes and couldn't believe the intensity of the orgasm. As I came, I felt his cock begin to swell. I didn't want this to end. This orgasm was humongous. The intensity was beyond pleasurable.

"Eight and a half!" I screamed.

He pulled his cock from my pussy.

Oh, so when I yell a number, he switches. Okay, I have this figured out.

"Stand up, Kelli," he said as he came to his feet.

I stood in front of him and smiled. My legs shook as I stood. He reached around my thighs and picked me up. I reached around his neck and held him in my arms as my legs dangled above the floor. He began walking toward the wall. When my back was a few inches from the wall, I knew what he was going to do.

Yaaaay! Wall sex. I love wall sex.

I lifted my legs and wrapped them around him. He forced himself into me. I pulled my legs as high as I could hold them and clenched my butt muscles. His hands were under my ass, holding me up.

He began fucking me hard. My back slapped against the wall as he thrust his cock inside of me. I closed my eyes. I love this sex. I feel powerless and like he is taking me. It makes me cum so hard. I like it when he is a little more forceful and my head hits the wall.

Moan, Kelli, moan.

I moaned.

"Ohhhhhh," I groaned.

He fucked me harder.

"Mmmmmm."

He fucked me harder. I opened my eyes and looked at his face. His jaw was clenched and he was in a zone. As I looked into his eyes, I moaned.

"Ohhhhh," I moaned as I smiled and looked into his eyes.

He began to slam his cock inside of me with tremendous force. My back slammed into the wall. He continued, his force increasing with almost every stroke. My head began to hit the wall. I moved my head toward his face. He pressed harder. My head hit the wall again. I released the tension in my neck.

Bang!

Bang!

Bang!

My head hit the wall as he fucked me. I closed my eyes. He forced his face between my collarbone and my face and bit my neck as he fucked me. I began to feel a wave of emotion over my entire body.

That's it, I'm done.

My pussy contracted and I came in three or four short, intense bursts. My body quivered. These orgasms were different. They were far more intense, but not as deep feeling. I loved these orgasms. I called them outside orgasms. He continued to fuck me. I had another. I opened my eyes. He clenched his jaw and fucked me into the wall.

Bang!
Bang!

I closed my eyes and focused on the feeling of his cock inside of me. In this position, it stayed in deep all the time with short forceful strokes. I felt his balls against my ass.

I closed my eyes.
Bang!
Bang!
Another intense orgasm.
And another.

I felt as if I was going to need to scream or run or break something. I couldn't take it anymore. These orgasms make me insane. I have to scream.

"Ten, fucking ten. Ten!" I screamed.

Shit, I said a word and not a number.

He exhaled and dropped me to the floor. My feet hit the floor, and my knees buckled. I collapsed onto the floor slowly. I leaned against the wall and relaxed. My entire body felt tingly. He looked down at me and caught his breath, his hands on his thighs.

"Put my cock in your mouth," he sighed.

Holy shit, I'm exhausted.

He took two steps toward me. I opened my mouth and raised my hands to grasp his cock.

"Put your fucking hands on your knees you little slut," he snapped.

I looked up at him and put my hands on my knees.

"Open your fucking mouth," he demanded.

Oh shit, I thought it was.

I opened my mouth.

He forced himself into my mouth. He didn't take it slow. I closed my eyes. He didn't go a half stroke. He immediately shoved his entire cock into my throat.

I'm not ready. Oh my God.

My throat convulsed and my stomach heaved. I swallowed quickly. I opened my eyes and looked up. He pressed his hips against my face, pressing me into the wall. He reached down and pinched my nipples as he fucked my face.

Bang!

Bang!

My head hit the wall as he fucked my face. He was taking short strokes, keeping his cock deep in my throat, and not pulling it out. My eyes watered. My throat convulsed. I felt like my lips were swelling. I felt smothered between him and the wall.

I can't breathe.

I raised my hands to his hips.

"Put those fucking hands down, you little bitch," he screamed.

I quickly shoved my hands back onto my knees and squeezed.

Bang!

Bang!

He forced himself deeper. And deeper. My eyes watered. Saliva dripped from my chin onto his feet. He slowly pulled his cock out of my mouth.

I gasped for air. *Thank God.* I opened my eyes and looked around the room. Everything was blurry.

Bang!

His hips pressed my face to the wall. His cock was smashed against my cheek. He held me against the wall. His knees pressed against my chest. He pulled his weight from my face. I looked up, my face covered in my own slobber from his cock on my face.

He grasped his cock in his hand.

Whack!

He slapped my face with his cock.

What the fuck?

Seriously?

Whack!

He slapped it again, hard.

Whack!

I raised my hands to my face.

"Put your hands down, god damn it, Kelli," he barked.

I put my hands on my knees.

Whack!

He slapped the other side. My face stung from the impact. I closed my eyes.

Whack!

He stopped. I kept my eyes closed.

"You little slut. I wish you'd be a good little girl for me. I really do. Do not open your fucking mouth. Do not speak. Are you going to be a good girl for me?" he asked.

I opened my eyes and nodded my head.

"Are you?" he asked.

Baby Girl III

I nodded.

"I sure hope so," he said, "I sure hope so."

He shook his head slowly from side to side.

God this turns me on when he talks like this. I felt myself tingling. I was regaining energy. I just needed time.

"Stand up, baby girl," he said.

Yaaaaay. I'm Baby girl again.

I jumped to my feet. My legs ached. Slowly, I straightened my knees.

"Give me a hug," he said.

I hugged him tight.

I'm not going to talk until he says I can. I don't know if this is over yet, and I want to make him so proud.

"Are you my baby girl?" he asked.

I nodded.

"Go in the kitchen and sit in the sink," he said as he pointed to the kitchen.

I leaned away from him and looked into his eyes. He wasn't smiling. His hand pointed to the kitchen.

"The sink, baby girl," he said sharply.

I walked to the kitchen. I looked at the sink. We had a large oversized sink with one large compartment instead of two. The water faucet had a sprayer on it that could be pulled from the faucet and used to wash vegetables or dishes – kind of like a removable shower nozzle.

I looked at the sink and turned my back to it. I grabbed the edge of the counter and hoisted myself to the countertop. Sitting on the edge of the countertop, I slid into the basin of the sink. Erik walked in behind me. As I sat in the sink, he looked at me and shook his head from side to side slowly.

He reached for the remote control, and turned up the Ipod. *Wax Tailor, How I Feel* played.

How appropriate. A new dawn, a new day, it's a new life for me... you know how I feel.

I felt like a chicken or something.

He walked to the sink and looked at me. He leaned toward my back and looked at my hair, back and arms.

"Close your eyes," he said.

I closed my eyes.

I felt his hand behind me. I heard him remove the nozzle from the faucet.

Shit.

He turned on the faucet and I heard it spray for a few seconds. I felt the water splash up against me. It changed from cold to warm. I felt small droplets against my thighs and butt as I heard it spray. I felt

85

SCOTT

his hand on my hair as he moved my hair from my face. He pulled it to the side of my face and massaged my scalp.

This is weird.

A short burst of water hit my chest. I jerked and opened my eyes.

"Keep your eyes closed, please," he said softly.

Shit, I forgot to say a number in the living room for him face fucking me and cock slapping me.

I reached up and pointed to toward the living room.

"Nine," I said as I pointed to the living room.

I put my hand back at my side. I relaxed and listened to the music. My legs ached from being stuffed into the sink.

Softly, he sprayed my hair. His hand caressed my scalp as he sprayed it from my scalp to the tips. As water hit my face, he wiped it away. The warm water felt good on my scalp. The tension in my legs went away and they quit aching. I relaxed and thought about the day we met in the dealership.

Erik with a "K", Enunciate Kelli.

I felt the warm water hit my chest. I smiled. His hand softly slid across my breast, squeezing lightly. His finger circled my nipple. I felt his mouth on my nipple. His tongue licked as his lips lightly kissed. His mouth moved away. I felt the water again. The water dripped down my stomach to between my legs. I could feel it pooling up at my crotch, where my thighs were pressed together.

I felt the water on my hair again. My scalp began to warm up. As he sprayed my hair lightly with the warm water, he kissed my lips lightly. His hand massaged my scalp as we kissed. My entire body tingled.

I have no idea where he gets these ideas, but he sure knows how to get in my head, and make me want to spend every day with him. Understanding him, figuring him out, learning what makes him tick. This man makes me insane. There cannot be another person on this earth like this. Some way, somehow, he knows exactly what to do and how to do it.

The water trickled down my face onto my chin. I squeezed my eyes together. He kissed my cheek. His tongue slid along my face to my chin. As he licked my chin, I felt his lips touch me. His mouth encompassed my chin and he kissed it. As he kissed it, he sucked the water off of it.

I felt his hands behind my shoulders as he slid his mouth to my neck. As he kissed my neck and shoulders, he pulled against my shoulders, leaning my upper body toward him.

His hands slid to under my armpits. He lifted my weight from the sink. I kept my eyes closed. As my legs slipped from the sink, he held my wet body to his and kissed me deep and long.

Our lips against each other, his tongue explored my mouth. He kissed my lips and pulled away. Immediately, he kissed me again, his tongue licking my lips as he began to kiss. As he kissed me, I felt his hands on my back pulling me against him. One hand slid to my ass and held squeezed. His hips against mine, I felt his cock rise against my thigh.

Our lips parted again. He kissed me gently and quickly twice as our bodies parted.

I kept my eyes closed.

I had to capture this and separate it from everything. Weird. Erotic. Nice. Fuck, I don't even know what this was.

"Ten," I said.

"Ten. Ten. Ten," I repeated.

I kept my eyes closed as he guided me across the floor. His hands slipped behind my thighs and around my shoulder. He picked me up from the floor and placed me on the countertop at the island.

"Lay down, baby girl," he said.

I laid flat on my back.

I heard him get onto the countertop at the end of the island. I felt his knees between my thighs. His chest pressed against mine, and we began to kiss again. As we kissed I spread my legs wider to invite him inside of me.

I felt his weight lift from my thighs and hips, and then felt the head of his cock against my wet pussy. Slowly, he slid inside.

"Mmmmmm," I moaned.

He kissed my lips as he slowly fucked me. His cock slid in and out slowly and deeply. I wrapped my arms around his back and pulled his chest against mine. He did not resist as I pulled him to me. I kept my eyes closed and rolled them back a little, enjoying the feeling of him being inside of me and against my chest.

Thank God. I love him against my chest.

As he continued to kiss me, his hips worked back and forth. The feeling of his cock inside of me was intense. Everything combined was more than I could take. His tongue licked my lips as his hand touched my face. His finger moved my wet hair to behind my ear. He lifted his mouth from my lips, and moved it to my ear.

"I love you baby girl. I love you with every ounce of my being. Understand that," he whispered into my ear.

His warm breath made me shiver.

His hips worked back and forth, and his cock filled me.

"Can you cum for me?" he breathed into my ear.

That's it. I'm done.

His breathing became more labored. He began to take quick short breaths.

I relaxed and focused on the feeling of his cock inside of me. I began to contract. As I did, he kissed me deeply. It felt as if his cock doubled in size. I felt it swell. I began to cum. Hard. A deep orgasm. An exhausting orgasm. The kind that puts you to sleep in the middle of the day. It came from my soul.

"Ohhhhhhh," I moaned as I came.

I bit my lip.

"Mmmmmmm," I moaned, my body tingling from head to toe, still cumming.

Slowly, his cock worked in and out. Then, he held it deep.

I felt him explode inside of me. His warm cum filled me as he squeezed my shoulder in his hand and kissed my lips lightly.

"I love you baby girl," he said as his cock twitched inside of me.

He kissed my lips.

"Open your eyes," he said.

I opened my eyes.

"You can talk now," he said.

I nodded.

"I love you," he said.

I opened my mouth and licked my lips slowly. I looked at his beautiful face. He was teaching me so much about myself. I loved this man like no other woman could ever experience. He was as unique as could be. He defined, to me, what perfection was. I looked up and down his tattooed, muscled body.

I sighed.

He smiled.

"Eleven," I said.

"A good solid eleven," I paused.

"And I love you back."

Chapter Fourteen

*E*RIK. "So how did it get so, well...critical?" I asked, my hands pressed tight to my hips.

"It's almost impossible to determine for sure, but he has about ten percent of the use of his remaining kidney. So, technically, he has five percent of what you have," the doctor explained.

"And the dialysis?" I asked, looking down at the floor.

"He's been on dialysis for three weeks. Some do well with dialysis, others not so well. I would have to check to be certain, but if memory serves me correctly, he's been three or four times a week," he said.

"What's the bottom line, doc?" I asked.

"He's dying, Erik. The dialysis causes anemia, the anemia is countered by the iron we're giving him, he's just...well, he's just *dying*," he responded in a very matter of fact tone.

"Wrong answer, doc. What can we do?" I asked.

"There's nothing that can be done now, it's just a matter of time," he responded again, looking at his watch.

"I appreciate you meeting me down here," I said as I extended my hand.

He extended his arm and shook my hand.

"I've got another..." he stammered, again looking at his watch.

"I understand. Again, thank you. I uhhmm...one thing. I need one thing," I said, turning to face him again.

"Yes?" he asked.

"I'm on the sheet. I'm listed as family, correct?" I asked.

He nodded before he looked at the screen of his iPad, "Yes here it is, Erik Ead. You are."

"Make note. If anything happens, you call me. Not Kelli. You call me. No exceptions, understand?"

SCOTT

"I'll make note of it," he said.

"Make note now, doc. Do it now," I demanded.

"Consider it done," he said as he scribbled on his pad.

"Thanks, doc," I said as he turned to walk away.

I walked out of the waiting room and turned down the hallway. I slowed my walk down and took my time. I was not looking forward to this. As I approached the room, I took a deep breath and exhaled.

I slowly opened the door. Kelli sat on the edge of the bed, looking at her father's face, whispering to him quietly. It was apparent she had been crying. She turned to face me, and quickly wiped her face, checking for tears.

I walked to the foot of the bed and reached down to touch Gene's feet. They felt cold. I covered them with the blanket and tucked it under his heels.

"Son, how you doing?" he asked in a raspy voice.

"I'm doing well, Gene. You need to get your ass out of here, the dealer is going to go to hell without you. They'll be giving cars away before you know it," I said, trying to change the mood a little.

"Get me a wheelchair in here. Hell, if you can fit me in the trunk of your M, we can skedaddle," he chuckled.

The chuckle produced a cough.

He was dying. He looked like a different man in a matter of a few weeks. Seeing him sickened me. I stood and wondered why I couldn't have his blood type. I would sacrifice all that I had for this man.

Time passes and things change.

That is a given.

Kelli held his hand and tried to force a smile.

"Kelli, let me talk to Erik for a minute. You want to go down to the cafeteria and get something for you two to drink?" Gene asked.

Kelli looked at me and then turned back to Gene. Slowly, she stood. She straightened the wrinkles from her jeans, leaned over and kissed his forehead.

"What...uhhmm. What," she coughed into her hand.

"Want. What do you want?" she asked as she walked toward me.

"Water, baby. Just a bottle of water," I responded.

She pulled her purse from the chair and put it over her shoulder. As she approached me, she stood on her tip-toes and puckered her lips. As I kissed her, she pulled her head back slowly and whispered.

"He's gonna be just fine," she said, "just fine."

I nodded and fought back tears, knowing otherwise.

After Kelli was gone, I walked to the head of the bed and held Gene's hand.

"Go make sure she's gone son," he said softly.

I walked to the door and opened it. I stepped into the hall and

Baby Girl III

looked both directions. The halls were bare, short of a lone nurse pushing a pill cart. I walked back into the room.

I nodded, "She's gone."

"What we talked about the other day. Take care of her. I need you to promise me, Erik. Again. Promise me. I know what you told me before we even talked, but there's a difference. Promise me," he muttered as he wiped his lips with the back of his hand.

"Gene, I promise," I said.

"Dry," he said, wiping his lips again.

I turned and looked at the bedside table. I grabbed the cup sitting there and pulled a few ice chips from the cup. I placed one of them in his mouth. He winked his eye. I placed another as soon as he was done with the first.

"You're a good man, son. You never fooled me. Act all tough to those pissy friends of yours, but I know better. You're a good kid. My daughter's lucky," he rasped.

"I've got a sale underway on the dealer. I'm going to sell it. I'm going to give you two the money. Kelli doesn't need to run that damned place to make me happy. You take care of her. That'll make me happy," he paused.

I placed another ice chip into his mouth.

"But it's your dream," I said.

"Mine, yes. Not hers. She has always wanted to make me happy. Making me happy would be living a productive life with someone that takes care of her and cherishes her, just like I have. You hurt that girl..."

I shook my head.

He slowly raised his hand.

"You hurt that girl and I'll come back from my grave and cut your dick off, son. Remember that. Clean off. You can bank on that, you hear me?" he asked.

"Yes sir," I responded.

"Don't mention the dealership to Kelli. She's convinced I'm going to get out of here. I haven't had the heart to tell her I only have one kidney yet. Can't decide if I should. It's tough son. It's just tough," he began to cough.

I squeezed his hand in mine.

"I may ask her if she wants to stay with me tonight. Maybe I will be able to muster the courage to talk to her. I really need to," he said.

I placed another ice chip in his mouth.

"Hell, you ought to be a caregiver, you big dumb monkey," he laughed.

His laughter caused another coughing fit.

I leaned into the bed, took the bottom of my tee shirt, and wiped his mouth. He winked at me again as I did. The door opened and

SCOTT

Kelli walked in with three bottles of water. She walked up to the bed and handed me one. She placed the other beside the bed on the bedside table.

"Baby, I need Erik to take care of some stuff for me at the dealer. You want to stay here with me tonight? I'll scooch to the side of the bed and make some room for ya," he said, smiling.

She looked at me for assurance. I nodded.

"Yes, daddy. I'd love to stay with you," she said.

"Scooch now," she said as she walked to the other side of the bed.

I grasped the blankets that were underneath Gene and pulled them in my direction, moving him to the side of the bed.

"Well, if I'm going to get that stuff done, I better get out of here, Gene," I said as I set the water on the table.

Kelli adjusted herself onto the bed beside her father, and laid down on her side. On top of the blankets, she scooted closer to him until her body was against his.

I walked to her side of the bed and leaned down to kiss her cheek.

"I love you, Kelli," I said.

"I love you back," she said.

"Thanks son. I love you," Gene said.

Two people other than the men I rode with were telling me they loved me, and I knew that they both meant it. This was new to me. New, but welcome.

"I love you too, Gene. I'll see you tomorrow," I said as I grabbed my water and walked to the door.

I opened the door and stepped half way through it. I turned back to face the room. I had something I wanted to say, but I wasn't sure what it was. Kelli raised her hand in the air, her palm open. As she did, her father raised his hand in the air slowly, his index finger extended. She grasped his finger in her hand and squeezed in into her palm.

And they both closed their eyes.

Chapter Fifteen

KELLI. I carried the ladder up the steps and into the kitchen. It was heavy and awkward to carry. I knew if I dropped it or drug it on the floor, Erik would notice, and I would be in trouble. I needed to get it up the steps and to our bedroom.

I gripped it tight in my hands and grunted as I started up the steps.

When I got into the bedroom, I set the ladder beside the bed and spread the legs apart. I stepped onto the rung and made sure it felt secure.

We all pray to the same God. Call him whatever you prefer. Allah. Buddha. God. It doesn't matter, there's one. We all believe in what we believe in. That belief gives us hope. It provides us with a form of power. The power of prayer is the power of belief. Belief that the prayer and who you're praying to will work.

The power of prayer. The power of thought. The power of hope. Some of the simplest things in life are the most powerful. From within our own self, when considering our experiences, we can find hope, strength, and comfort in living and believing. Believing is solving.

We all need *something* to believe in.

Erik had told me of the talisman. It had been blessed and was not to be touched. He said it was blessed and was to provide him with protection from harm. Not a good luck charm so to speak, but a medallion of a powerful nature. It was something that could protect him from bad coming into his life. It would also protect people that he loved, because people that he loved being hurt would hurt him. That was my guess anyway.

The talisman was not to be touched by anyone. If someone touched it, it would absorb all of the bad that is within them, and then it would not provide Erik with the protection and the good that was intended. Only if Erik trusted the person one hundred percent could he ever let them touch it. They had to be pure, and never intend on bringing him bad. They had to be a person that had Erik's best interest as their best interest.

I looked up at the ceiling and climbed the ladder. When I got to the top and leaned toward the medallion, I shook. Not from the ladder being insecure, but from something else. I reached out toward the talisman and hesitated. I closed my eyes and thought.

I have no choice.

I reached for it and grasped it into my hand. The metal of it felt cold. As I held it, I felt an odd feeling of three people being in the room. Erik, my father, and I.

Three.

I closed my eyes and prayed.

God, if you're listening, I have to talk to you. I need a favor, God. I'm not really sure how to do this, but I know you don't want lip service from me. I'm not going to make you promises. I'm not going to change my life if you do some miracle for me. I just want to talk.

I clutched the medallion in my hand and held it close to my heart.

God, my father is sick. You know that. He is a child of yours so you know. I ask that you stop and take a look at him for a minute. He's a great man. He took care of me for my entire life, and he did a good job. I grew up and I made bad decisions. Me. I made them. If he knew some of the things that I did, he would skin me alive. But the decisions were mine.

He raised me well.

God, he needs help. I am asking you in the name of Jesus, that you consider giving him what it is that he needs to survive. I know that he can't live forever, but you can make him live for a while. Just a little while longer. I have a plan, God, and he's part of it. Just take a look at him and see what you can do.

One more thing, God. For whatever reason, you put Erik in my life.

Thank you for that.

I squeezed the talisman in my hand and opened my eyes. I looked around the room. I closed my eyes and continued.

I know holding this thing may seem weird to you God, but it's all I have. I wanted to be as close to you as I could be, and I felt that this was the best for us both. If Erik is in my life to replace my father, I guess that you made a good choice. Erik loves me, I know he does. I ask that you bless him too, God. Keep him healthy. I can't survive on this earth alone, and do it as good as I can with him. Keep him healthy, please.

Help me make all good decisions, God.

I try so hard to do whatever it is that is good, but we all make mistakes. Help me make as few of them as possible.

Please look after all of Erik's brothers. You know who they are. They're good men, God. They are.

God, if you decide to take my father, I cannot change that. I guess if you take him from me and from this earth, please take care of him; because he is a special man. He is a good man. He's my daddy.

God, I ask that you take care of him so when Erik and I get to Heaven he will be in good health for us. We both love him so much. I hate seeing him sick.

I know you'll do whatever your plan is. Whatever it is, help me understand it.

Understand it and accept it.
In your name I pray.
Amen.
And.
Thank you.

Chapter Sixteen

*E*RIK. There are two kinds of phone calls that are received at three o'clock in the morning. It is either bad news or a wrong number. When the phone rang, I was hoping for the latter. What I got was not what I wanted, nor was it what I was ready for.

I switched the light on and placed the phone back on the top of the dresser.

"Kelli, wake up," I said as I shook her.

"Kelli," I shook her again.

"Huh? What's going on," she rolled over, squinted, and looked at me as if she were lost.

"Get up, baby girl, we need to go," I said as I put on my jeans.

"Why?" she asked, still wrapped into the blankets.

"Baby, we have to run to the hospital," I said softly.

"Why? What time is it?" she asked as she rubbed her eyes.

"Baby, it's 3:16 in the morning," I responded as I looked at my watch.

She sat up in bed and rubbed her eyes again.

"What's going on," she asked.

"Baby, it's your father. We need to go. *Now*," I demanded softly as I pulled my shirt over my head.

"Okay," she got out of bed and wandered to the closet.

She stepped out of the closet in a pair of sweats and a tee shirt.

"Get some shoes, baby girl," I said.

"I'll wear my slippers. He's going to be alright," she said, nodding her head slowly.

"Baby, he's really sick. We need to go," I said as I walked to the doorway.

"He's going to be fine," she said as she shuffled to catch up to me.

SCOTT

Witnessing Kelli's denial of her father's impending death was probably no different than my friends watching for years as I denied the fact that my mother was dead. It made me sick to think about Kelli's father dying. In the short period of time that I had come to know him, he meant a tremendous amount to me. In addition to being Kelli's father, he was a damned good man. I was disappointed that I hadn't known him longer.

The doctor stated that he was dying and we needed to get to the hospital post haste. There was question of whether or not he would live until daylight. His kidney had failed totally a few days prior and the dialysis was not going well. His body had finally shut down and other organs were now in question.

"He's going to be fine, isn't he?" she asked as I backed the car out of the driveway.

"Kelli, it's hard to say," I responded.

I didn't know what else to tell her. I turned on the bright beams and sped up down the road toward the city. I turned off the music so we could talk on the way. Kelli stared intently out the window of the car into the darkness.

"Baby, we just need to be prepared for the worst," I said softly as I drove.

She turned to face me.

"Like an operation, you mean?" she asked.

"Baby, I don't know. *Something*," I responded.

She wasn't making this any easier.

As we drove along the street to the hospital, I gripped the steering wheel and clenched my jaw. I looked into the dark star filled sky. And...

I did something I had not done since I was a kid.

I prayed.

Looking through the windshield into the starry sky, I squinted my eyes and spoke to my inner mind.

And to God.

My world is crumbling before my eyes and I don't know what else to do. I'm sure, in a world of perfection, we would all come to you in times of bliss, and not merely in times of sorrow and guilt.

We haven't spoken in thirty years. I don't ask for much, so it would stand to reason when I do, you may listen. I am asking if you have the method and the means that you do so with a keen ear.

One man, God.

One.

There's one man right now that you need to be aware of. His name is Gene Parks. He's dying. I know in my heart of hearts that you will be better served with this man on earth and not with you.

I'm not here to barter, trade, or make some sort of deal. I'm not going to promise to worship you to a greater degree if you grant my wishes expressed in prayer. I'm here to ask your consideration. That's all.

Take a look in this man's eyes. If you don't see the most caring, loving, and compassionate human being you've ever produced…well, so be it.

But if you're half as intelligent as I am, and I'm certain you are; you'll see what I see.

A man that has been instrumental in the development of the love that is before you now. In his eyes, God, his two children are before you now. I pray, God, that whatever happens…whatever it is that may be your will – please provide Kelli and I with the strength to understand and accept it.

That is all I ask. Amen.

I looked over into the passenger seat. Kelli was asleep, slumped over onto the door. I reached over and softly placed my hand on her leg and held it there. As I turned into the hospital parking lot, her weight shifted and she woke up.

"We're here?" she asked as she rubbed her eyes.

I nodded. A lump rose in my throat.

"That didn't take long," she said.

I tried unsuccessfully to swallow.

"Well, come on," I said as I opened the door.

Kelli wrapped her arm around mine and shuffled her feet as we walked through the lot. As her slippers scraped through the sand in the parking lot, I continued my brisk pace toward the door.

"Slow down, I'm going to lose my slippers," she said softly as she looked down at her feet.

"Kelly, we need to…" I paused.

"Okay, baby girl. I'm sorry," I said as I slowed my pace.

As the elevator rose to the third floor, my mind filled with emotion. Wonder, hope, fear, and sorrow consumed me. Kelli stood, stone faced and held my arm in hers. I turned and looked at her. As I did, she looked up and smiled.

The elevator door opened and we walked down the hall to room where Gene had been. I slowly pushed the door open, prepared for the worst.

The room was empty.

"Where is he?" Kelli asked.

I started to open my mouth, but realized I could not come close to speaking. I shrugged my shoulders and swallowed.

I turned and walked toward the reception desk, Kelli in tow. The nurse at the desk was tapping on a keyboard and made no effort to look up when we approached.

"Gene Parks," I said, "where is he?"

"Just one moment, please," she said as she typed.

I reached over the counter and placed my hand over the computer screen. She turned and looked up at my face. I clenched my teeth and flexed my jaw muscles.

"*We don't have a minute*. He was here, and he's gone from his room. Dialysis patient. Sixty-four years old. We received a call, we need to know where he is," I said sternly.

I moved my hand from the screen.

She typed on the keyboard and looked at the screen and squinted.

"AICU, on seven. 724," she said.

"Thank you," I whispered.

"Why'd they move him, Erik?" Kelli asked.

"Hard saying, baby," I said as we walked back toward the elevator.

I pushed the button for the seventh floor and closed my eyes.

The door dinged when it reached the seventh floor.

I hope you were listening earlier.

I opened my eyes.

We walked into the circular shaped room. I looked at the room numbers above the doors and followed the numbers until we reached room 724.

I slid the curtain that covered the doorway into the room. The bed was unkempt, but the room was empty. I scanned the room. The board on the wall beside the bed had the name *Parks* written on it.

I turned back into the hallway.

"What's going on, Erik?" Kelli asked.

I shrugged.

"Ma'am, where's the man that was in this room? Gene Parks?" I asked a passing nurse.

"Let me get someone for you," she said.

As she hurriedly walked toward the reception desk, we followed her. It wasn't shocking to me that Kelli had become very quiet. Even considering her typical silent submissive nature, she was extremely quiet for the last few days. Fear, denial, and being filled with wonder probably prevented her from speaking much. Tonight she was even quieter than she had been for the last few days. She held my arm as we walked to the desk.

The nurse whispered to another nurse who was sitting at the desk. The nurse at the desk stood and walked from behind the desk and stood in front of us.

"There were some complications with anemia," she said, and took a deep breath.

"And for some reason, during treatment, he went into anaphylactic shock," she paused again.

"*Anaphylactic shock?* How in the *fuck* did he go into anaphylactic shock? What did you give him?" I demanded.

"Sir, we. Well. I'm not sure, we..." she stammered.

"Jesus fucking Christ," I shook my head, "he had severe reaction to an antigen. Someone introduced it. What was it? What happened? Where is he?"

She pointed toward the entrance.

"Go to the waiting room in the hallways on the left, by the elevator. You passed it on your way in. I will get a doctor to see you as soon as I can. He's down the hallway with a few doctors, but you can't go in there," she said.

"How long? How long will *you* keep us waiting?" I asked, attempting to make her feel responsible to get a doctor to us as soon as possible.

"As soon as I can. I cannot interrupt them, but I will get a doctor to, and get someone to see you as soon as possible," she promised.

"What does all of that mean, Erik?" Kelli asked as we sat on the waiting room couch.

I inhaled a slow breath through my nose and exhaled through my mouth.

"When an *antigen* is introduced to your body, say when you get a vaccine shot, are given an antibiotic, or anything that isn't normally in your body, your body naturally creates an antibody. The antibody renders the foreign substance harmless. Sometimes the reaction to the antigen is severe, and your body goes into shock," I inhaled another breath and thought.

"Like a bee sting, baby. When someone is allergic to a bee sting," I explained.

Kelli nodded.

"So they gave daddy something he was allergic to?"

"Basically, yes," I responded, knowing the anaphylactic shock could kill him in no time, and that it wasn't the reason we were called here.

I placed my hands on my knees and rocked slowly into the seat of the couch. Kelli leaned over toward my shoulder and laid her head on my upper arm. Soon, I heard her breathing change. I looked over my shoulder and confirmed she was asleep. I closed my eyes and relaxed. This to me was exhausting.

"Your father is in the car waiting, Erik," my mother said.

I walked out the front door onto the porch and looked into the driveway. He rolled down the window and waved his arm.

"Don't forget your bat and glove, son," he shouted, pointing to the porch.

I looked down and noticed the glove and baseball bat by the doorway. Quickly, I grabbed them and ran for the car. The trunk to the car was opened, and I threw my bat and glove in the trunk, closed it, and got into the rear seat of the car.

"Buckle your seatbelt," he said as I sat into the seat.

I buckled my seatbelt and leaned forward to catch a glimpse of his face. The seatbelt restricted me from leaning forward far enough. I leaned back into the seat and sighed.

"So, you going to hit a homer, son?" he asked.

"I'll sure try," I answered, filled with wonder.

"That last game was a doozy. That pop fly you caught won the game as far as I see it," he said.

"Me too," I said.

"You sure run the bases well. Good strong legs on you, son," he said.

"Thank you, sir," I said attempting again to lean forward.

The seat belt caught me half way to the rear of the front seat.

"Son, sit still. If we get into a wreck, that seat belt will save your life, but only if you're sitting in the seat properly," he said.

"Yes sir," I responded.

He turned the corner and accelerated up the on ramp to the highway. I watched out the windows as the cars passed us. Soon, he was up to the same speed as traffic. I listened to the repetitive whump whump whump of the tires on the road below and closed my eyes.

"We'll be there in a few minutes, son. You're going to need to be alert. Your game is the first one today," he said.

"Yes sir," I said as I opened my eyes.

The car changed lanes, and began to slow down. We exited the highway and sped down the exit ramp toward the stop light. The light was red. I felt the car begin to decelerate. As the light turned green, the car accelerated again, and headed for the intersection.

"Can't wait for this game, it should be a damn fine display, Centre Park's team is a good one son," he said over his right shoulder.

"That's what they're saying," I said, smiling.

I saw the truck coming, but I couldn't speak. As we entered the intersection, he turned around, but there was no time. Even seeing the truck approaching, the explosion startled me. As we passed through the intersection, the truck hit the driver's side door, causing the car to flip over. It tumbled several times before it came to a stop.

I looked around the car. Glass was everywhere. The smell of smoke filled the car. The airbags in the front were out like huge balloons. My father was slumped into the seat.

"Dad?" I screamed.

"Dad!"

I tried to open my door. It wouldn't budge. I pulled the handle and kicked it as hard as I could. As I kicked it, it opened half way. I stepped out into the street, and around to the driver's door of the car. People were stopping and walking up to the car.

The driver's door was mangled, and the entire driver's side of the car was destroyed. A lifeless body lay slumped in the seat. A man reached in and placed his hand on my father's neck.

"Does anyone know CPR?" he screamed.

"Anyone?" he screamed again.
"Call an ambulance!" he shouted.
"Someone call an ambulance!"
I looked around at the people as they all talked to each other. One ran to a drug store on the corner. The trunk to the car was open. I walked to the rear of the car and looked inside. My bat and glove were still inside. I reached in and picked them up.

"Someone, Jesus. Someone please, call an ambulance," the man screamed.
Clutching my ball and bat, I walked to the curb and sat down.
I clutched my ball and bat close to my chest and waited.
For an ambulance that never arrived.

"Mr. Eads?" a hand touched my shoulder.

I grabbed the wrist firmly and opened my eyes.

"Mr. Eads?" he asked again.

"There's no "s", it's Ead. Erik Ead," I said as I sat up on the couch.

Kelli slumped into the couch beside me, obviously asleep. I stood and motioned for him to step beside the couch. I needed to protect her from as much of this as possible.

"Yes sir?" I said.

I noticed it was daylight as he began to take a deep breath. I looked at my watch. 8:14. I had been asleep quite a while. I looked up from my watch and into the doctor's eyes.

"Well, it's been a hell of a night. We had complications from anemia, and when we…"

"Bottom line, doc. Just cut the horseshit, what's the bottom line," I demanded.

He stopped speaking and looked shocked. I turned to look at Kelli, who was still asleep on the couch. I turned back to face the doctor.

"Dead or alive, which is it?" I asked.

"Well, he's alive. As you know, his kidney has failed completely. We thought last night we were going to lose him twice, but…" he paused.

"Well. Life is full of mysteries, I suppose. Mysteries and surprises, Mr. Ead. He in no way is doing *well*, he's as close to death as he can be and still be living. The operation is not something that we would *normally* perform with him in this condition, but we have no choice. We're going to attempt it," he rubbed his hands on his thighs.

"Operation?" I asked.

"Yes, the kidney," he said.

"What are you going to do with it," I asked, knowing that it could not be repaired.

"There's been a donor, Mr. Ead. It's taken considerable time to complete all of the tests, but there's been an individual come forth.

SCOTT

Somewhat unique circumstances, but a donor none-the-less," he smiled as he spoke.

I stood straight and attempted to speak. A lump rose in my throat. I wiped a tear from my eye and tried again.

Nothing.

I held my finger in the air and wiped my eyes free of tears with my free hand.

"Just a..." my voice cracked.

"Just a second."

I raised both hands to my face and wiped my tears.

I knew you were listening.

"Who?" I asked, standing there shaking.

"The individual wants to remain anonymous," he stated as he rubbed his hands together.

"When?" I asked excitedly.

"It's underway now. It's going to be several hours more. Maybe you should sleep or get some food. He's down on three in the O.R., when you're ready you ought to go to the waiting room there," he said.

I nodded. I was still trying to process all of this.

"The elevator here down to three, and follow the hallway all the way on the right side to the sign that says Operating Room Waiting. It's a long way, don't get discouraged," he said.

I nodded.

He took a breath and exhaled, still rubbing his hands together.

"You realize this is complicated at best?" he asked.

"Yes sir," I responded.

"There are no assurances. He's in extremely poor health," he said.

"I understand, do all you can," I paused and then finished what I'd waited a lifetime to say.

"Because he's the only father I've got."

Chapter Seventeen

KELLI. Being with Erik made life simple. He made me feel like I had nothing to worry about. Ever. He made me feel like a woman. He made me feel like a child. He made me feel secure.

I took a chance with Erik and he took a chance with me. Wayne Gretzky said, *You miss a hundred percent of the shots you don't take.*

Wayne was right.

Erik was proving every day that he was so much more inside than what he was on the surface. And on the surface, he was magnificent.

"*Park Place.* Ha fucking ha," he said as he moved his top hat along the outside of the board.

"Are you thirty-six, or ten?" I asked.

"Park Place is prime real estate," he said, smiling.

I shook my head and held my hand out for the dice. As he handed them to me, he leaned over the board and kissed me.

"I love you, baby girl," he said.

Melting.

"I love you back," I responded as he handed me the dice.

"I'm going to own your little ass," he said as he pointed to the Monopoly board.

"You already do," I responded.

I took a drink of my coffee and shook the dice in my other hand.

"*Ead. Erik Ead,*" the doctor bellowed as he walked into the waiting room.

"Stay here, Kelli. I'll be right back," he said as he stood up.

Erik walked to the far end of the waiting room and approached the doctor.

Erik told me he would talk to all of the doctors, because he could understand them better than I could. They talked to him, and he talked to me. I liked it that way. Erik took care of me. They were operating on my daddy, and giving him a new kidney. Erik said it was a complicated operation, and that it took a long time. We had eaten breakfast, and now we were playing Monopoly. I love Monopoly. The game had been going on for hours.

Erik stood and talked to the doctor for a moment, wiped his face, and then shook the doctor's hand. He turned from the doctor, wiped his face with again with both hands, and walked back to the table.

"Progress report," I said as I looked up and into his face.

"They're done. It's over," he said and then took a breath.

"Your father has a new kidney. He'll be in recovery for a while, and then we can go see him," he said, standing over me.

I shook the dice in my hand.

"Did you hear me?" he asked.

I nodded my head.

"Uh huh, my turn," I said as I tossed the dice on the board.

"Seven. One, two, three, four, five, six, seven. Crap. *Go To Jail.*" I whined.

Erik walked up to his seat and pulled it out from the table.

"I knew he was going to be okay," I said.

"Oh?" he asked.

"Uh huh, I said a special prayer," I admitted as I handed Erik the dice.

"So did I," he said.

"*So did I.*" he said again as he tossed the dice.

Chapter Eighteen

*K*ELLI. Any woman with half of a heart would fall in lust with Erik Ead in a matter of minutes of being exposed to him. Initially, I fell in *lust*. Now, I sat in the kitchen as madly in love with him as any woman could be in love with anyone. No one could know Erik, actually know him, and *not* love him. Underneath that hard outer shell, he was as caring of a human being as has ever graced this earth.

People who don't know of our relationship and our sexual preferences say Erik is cruel because of the sex that we practice. Erik is giving me what I want because he loves me. If I didn't want it, he wouldn't do it. He guides me, protects me, provides me with assurance, and explains things to me that I do not understand. He never mistreats me, or abuses me morally, mentally, or physically. He never harms me, or forces me to do anything I do not want to do.

Exclude the sex from our relationship, and Erik Ead is an angel.

An angel covered in muscles and tattoos.

He stood in front of the stove and made breakfast while I sipped coffee. He was wearing sweats, slippers, and no shirt. As he reached for the batter his bicep flexed and his back muscles twitched.

Squuueeeeeee.

"Put on a shirt," I said as I sipped my coffee.

Paul Thorn, Ain't Love Strange played on the Ipod.

He looked over his right shoulder and squinted.

"Please?"

"You know I hate wearing shirts in the house, especially in the morning before I shower," he responded.

"I can't take it anymore. New house rule in my half of the house. Wear a shirt, or…" I tapped my finger on my lip and thought.

"Or fuck me if it's off," I said.

He laughed out loud.

"You said the first time we were in here, the night we broke in – that I could never wear a shirt again, ever," he said over his shoulder.

He held up his arm and flexed his bicep.

Sweet baby Jesus.

"Things change. Rules change," I responded.

"You're adorable," he said as he flipped the pancakes.

A small saucepan warmed up fresh maple syrup that Shakey brought back from a trip. I was excited to eat Erik's special wheat pancakes and fresh syrup, but right now his biceps flexing, his back muscles twitching, and every available inch of his biker persona being covered in tattoos was just too much.

"I designate the kitchen *mine*," I said as I stood from the chair.

"Yours?" he giggled.

"Yep. Mine. Prepare for the wrath of me," I said as I walked his direction.

"You see me shaking?" he asked as he set the pancakes onto a plate with the others.

He covered the plate in aluminum foil.

"You'll be shaking soon enough," I laughed as I approached him.

He held the bowl of batter over the stove and reached for the spoon. I wedged myself between his waist and the stove. As he opened his arms to allow me room, I stood on my tip toes and kissed him.

"I love you, baby girl. Now scoot," he said as he waved his hand that held the spoon.

Batter dripped onto my arm. I looked at the batter droplets and back at him. As he watched intently, I wiped the batter with my fingertip. I licked the batter from the tip of my finger with as much eroticism as I could. It tasted unnaturally sweet.

Leaning backward, still allowing me room to be between him and the stove, he stood and stared with his mouth open. He held the bowl in his left hand, and the wooden batter covered spoon in his other.

I reached for the bowl and shoved my hand into the batter. As I pulled it out, batter dripped to the floor from my fingers.

"Kelli, what the *fuck*?" he asked as he shook his head and attempted to pull the batter away.

I slowly bent my knees. As I did, my chest pressed against his legs. I cupped my right hand close to my chest.

"Scoot. Isn't that what you said? *Scoot*," I said as I pushed against his legs with my elbow.

"What the fuck are you..." he began to ask.

I cupped the batter in my right hand. As he stepped back, I

grabbed the waist of his sweats with my left hand and yanked. They came down just far enough for his cock to flop out.

Perfect.

I grabbed his cock with my batter covered right hand and stroked it slowly. The batter was slippery. I stroked his cock until it was rigid. I cupped his smoothly shaved balls in my hand and covered them in batter. I pulled my hand back and slowly licked my fingers, looking up at him as I did.

He set the bowl on the counter and turned off the stove.

He reached for the remote control and turned up the music. *Ben Harper, Brown Eyed Blues.*

He wants this as much as I do.

"My kitchen, my rules," I said before I swallowed half of his batter covered cock.

I pulled my mouth from his cock, looked up at him, and licked my lips

"*Our* kitchen," he said.

"My kitchen, your hallway," I said, looking up at him.

I winked and took his entire cock into my mouth. My throat convulsed. I held his cock deep and pressed against the shaft with my tongue. Slowly, I released his cock from my mouth. I sucked hard as I did. When it passed my lips, it made a *pop*.

"Mine," I said, "wear a shirt or get naked," I said as I opened my mouth and guided his cock toward my lips.

"*Ours*. No shirt. I never wear a…"

I grabbed his ass in my left hand and took his entire length into my mouth. I took his cock into my throat and quickly slid back up the shaft. He gasped. I took it into my throat again. I closed my eyes. I released it. I took it into my throat again then released it. I squeezed his ass in my hand, and took his cock into my throat and held it. I opened my eyes and looked up. My throat convulsed. I pressed harder. I stretched my tongue out and licked his batter covered balls. He groaned. Slowly, I slid my mouth from his cock.

"Who's kitchen? Who *owns* this kitchen?" I asked, smiling.

The music changed to R. L. Burnside, Someday Baby.

There's no way he won't fuck me now.

He looked down and slowly smiled.

"Fuck it, baby girl. This kitchen's *yours*. Come here. *Now*," he said as he reached down and placed his hands under my arm pits.

He hoisted me to my feet.

"You're *always* gonna be trouble aren't you," he laughed as he lifted me to the island -referencing the song's lyrics, *someday baby you ain't gonna be trouble for me anymore.*

I nodded.

I loved this kitchen. I loved it when he brought me in her the first time. That was so hot. Every time I stepped into the kitchen I got wet. This house is perfect for us.

"Your kitchen, your rules. But now it's sex, and when it's sex, who calls the shots?" he asked.

"The shot caller," I responded, sitting on the island facing him.

"Who's the shot caller?" he asked as he spread my knees apart.

I pointed at his chest, "You sir."

"That's right. Don't forget it," he said as he turned toward the sink.

"Relax, baby girl, I'm going to wash the batter off my cock so you don't get a yeast infection," he laughed.

I leaned back onto my elbows and watched as he shuffled to the sink. He pulled his slippers off and kicked them aside. He pulled his sweats down and kicked them toward his slippers.

And as he stood there naked, washing his cock in the kitchen sink, I realized that my life with him was going to be full of interest, full of sexual surprise, and would never, ever get boring. Erik was right. The sexual diversity of a Dominant submissive relationship would keep half of the people together that eventually grow apart.

Tab Benoit, If I Could Quit You came on the Ipod. I closed my eyes and listened. I lowered myself onto the island countertop and relaxed. I heard Erik's soft footsteps on the floor. He turned the music up louder.

I smiled and kept my eyes closed.

I felt something really warm on my breasts. The feeling moved to my stomach and stopped at my belly button. I opened my eyes. Eric was pouring the fresh warm syrup from the saucepan onto my stomach.

Oh God.

"Your kitchen, my rules *now*," he said as he set the saucepan on the counter by the sink.

He began to lick my nipples as he squeezed my breasts lightly in his hands.

"Mmmm. This is *good*," he said as he sucked and licked each nipple.

I rose up onto my elbows and watched him suck and lick me. Watching his tongue glide across my syrup covered skin was more than I could take. I started to tingle. His mouth moved to my stomach and focused on the cavity of my belly button, which was filled with syrup. He slurped it from my stomach.

As he sucked and licked the syrup, his right hand slowly wiped across my stomach and across my torso to my breast. I watched as his fingers slid gracefully across my nipple to my neck. He maintained eyes contact as he lifted his fingers and held them over my mouth. I extended my tongue and licked his fingers. The sweet syrup was somewhat erotic in my mouth. I sucked his fingers one by one, taking them deep into my mouth slowly and sucking them syrup free.

Wax Taylor, Say Yes started to play as he pulled his fingers slowly from my mouth.

His mouth moved to my swollen wet pussy. His tongue darted across my clit. He licked as he pressed his mouth hard against me, pressing my clit between his tongue and his upper lip. He repeated the process over and over. I closed my eyes tightly and focused.

Don't. Stop. Doing. That.

"Erik…"

"Erik, I'm…"

"Oh God, Erik…please…."

"Cum, I'm going to…Oh…"

I raised my hips and moaned. He licked and sucked. I moaned again and thrust my hips toward his face. He slurped and sucked. He pressed his face hard into my pussy and forced his tongue in deep. I opened my eyes. I moaned.

And.

I came.

"Oh my fucking God…"

I opened and closed my eyes. I opened them again. I closed them and relaxed, uncertain of what happened.

He continued to lick as I wiggled. The sensitivity was insane. The syrup, his tattooed body, the muscles, and of the waiting were more than I could take. I was at the height of climax now. He licked my clit as he slid his finger in and out of my now soaked pussy. He added another finger. His tongue worked magically across my swollen clit. I began to tingle. I felt as if I was going to explode.

He started to moan as he licked and sucked. The moaning sent a sensation through my entire body. His tongue worked my clit as his finger slid in and out of my wet pussy.

Holy fuck I'm going to die.

"Stop moaning, I think…" I muttered.

He moaned louder as he licked and sucked.

"Erik, I think…"

He moaned and worked his fingers deeper.

"Oh my fucking God," I stuttered

I opened my eyes and looked down. He was watching me, his eyes wide open. He winked at me. *Oh fuck.* I tried to breathe. I couldn't. I inhaled and almost choked. My breathing became stuttered. I felt as if this was going to be my last breath. My heart rose into my throat. I tingled down deep in my soul. He sucked, licked, and moaned.

And I released.

SCOTT

I came. And came. I worked my hips, thrusting myself into his mouth.

He moaned as he licked.

And I came.

"Stop, please," I begged.

"I can't take it, don't touch me," I whispered.

He stood up and flexed his chest.

Dear God.

He grasped his cock in his left hand and started stroking it. I pushed myself up onto my elbows a little further. Standing there smiling, he continued to stroke his cock, the speed increasing as he stroked it. He flexed his biceps and made his pectoral muscles jump up and down.

Kill me now, please.

He reached toward the countertop and grabbed the saucepan of syrup in his right hand. I watched intently as he held it in front of his chest and poured the pan onto his shoulders, chest, and stomach. The syrup ran down to his cock and around to his thighs. As it touched his thighs, he flexed his muscles.

Is this really happening?

He took a few steps toward the island, raised his knees to the top, and jumped up onto the counter, straddling me. The syrup glistened on his smoothly shaven skin. I licked my lips. He crawled across the counter on his knees until his chest was over my face. As he lowered his massive tattooed chest to meet my lips, I moaned.

I can't take this anymore. I felt my wetness running into the crack of my ass.

I began to lick and suck his chest. The sweet syrup encouraged me to be more aware of where I was licking. His knees on either side of my thighs, I sucked and bit his nipples as I reached around his waist to support myself. His hands grasped my head lightly and pulled it tight to his chest.

I moaned as I licked his chest.

"Lean back," he said softly.

I leaned back onto my forearms, lowering my back closer to the counter. He lowered himself along my torso, dragging his chest along my nipples as he did. The sensation sent tingles through my spine. My body shuddered.

Please, Erik. Fuck me.

He leaned back on his knees as he held my head in his hands. He raised his knees and stood crouched on his feet, his stiff cock standing straight up. He worked the tip toward my face. As I opened my mouth he pulled my head onto the shaft with force. His cock forced itself into my throat. I coughed as it slid down deep. I opened my eyes and looked up. The sticky syrup pressed up against my face.

Baby Girl III

He held my head there for a moment and slid his cock free of my mouth.

As he lowered my head back to the countertop, he shifted his weight to his knees. His mouth met mine and as he kissed my lips lightly, he guided the tip of his swollen cock inside of me. As soon as it slid into my pussy, I began to contract.

"Erik," I gasped.

"Shhhh," he whispered as he kissed me.

He slowly worked himself in and out of my pussy. His chest pressed against mine. The warmth of his body pressed against me. We were stuck together by a thin film of syrup. It was a sensation that words can't describe. He kissed me as his hips worked slowly, softly biting my upper lip with each kiss. I felt myself start to tingle.

I felt frail underneath his massive upper body. I felt small. I felt protected. I felt *loved*.

"Erik, I'm going to…" I heaved for another breath.

I dug my fingernails into his back, grabbing for security. I felt as if I were going to explode. His breathing became labored and his chest heaved.

He licked my upper lip as his cock slid slowly inside of me.

"Erik…I," I took a breath.

"I'm going to cum." I exhale two short breaths.

"I'm going to cum so….hard," I gasped.

His breathing became more labored and his cock swelled.

Oh my God, he's going to cum already?

"Shhh," he said as he slid inside slowly.

And as he held his cock deep inside of me, I began to cum. Hard. My fingernails dug deeper into his skin and tore across his back. He arched his back and moaned, partially from pain, and mostly from the pleasure. His tongue licked my lips.

And he erupted inside of me. As he did, he moaned a moan of pleasure, holding his cock deep inside of me, arching his back.

I convulsed, my entire body tingling from an orgasm from deep within my soul. As he held himself deep inside of me, he moved his lips from mine.

"I love you, Kelli," he said as he looked into my eyes.

Erik Ead defines beautiful.

I have no idea what was different. What changed, or what may have happened.

But.

I opened my mouth and tried to speak. And I could not. His eyes glistened. My lips parted again slowly. *Nothing.*

With a heart filled with love.

And a mind full of emotion.

My eyes filled with tears.

SCOTT

As a tear ran down my cheek, he reached out to wipe it.
And I tried again.
"I love you…" I muttered.
He wiped my tears.
"Back," I said.

Chapter Nineteen

*E*RIK. Those that give and those that take. The world is full of both. The selfish and the selfless. There are always those that are willing to perform a selfless act and ask that no one acknowledge them for doing so. They don't do it for the praise, recognition, or any form of benefit other than the knowledge that they have helped someone that was incapable of helping themselves. They do it, because in their mind, it needs to be done. They see no other choice.

Soldiers, Sailors, Airmen, and Marines that give their lives. The man that leaves six gold coins at the Salvation Army during Christmas. We all want to thank them, and anyone that gives when other people only want to take.

But.

We can't always do so. We don't always know who they are, we only know that they exist. For their existence, always, I am grateful.

Today much more than others.

"And who, son, made you the fucking rule maker," he asked.

"God damn it, Gene, you're going to the car in a wheelchair," I said in a soft tone.

"Fuck you, I'm walking," he snarled.

"No you're not, you don't need to be walking," I said softly.

"Daddy, maybe Erik is right. We don't want you back in here for Thanksgiving," Kelli said.

"I should have known you'd side with him, god fucking damn. Fine. But I can tell you one god damned thing. When I get home, and you two fucktards are gone, I'm going to run around the god damned block," he said angrily.

"I haven't felt this good in fifty years. I feel like a fucking teenager," he said, quickly shuffling his feet back and forth.

SCOTT

"Gene, I'm glad you feel better, but this is ridiculous. You're still in recovery," I said.

"True, but I have a new kidney.. Shit, they said this thing was thirty years newer than me. I want to run a foot race and fuck a wild cat," he said.

"Daddy!" Kelli screamed.

"Sorry, baby. I forgot you were here," he smiled.

"Fine, I'll let you wheel me out of here, you big arrogant prick," he said as he sat on the edge of the bed.

The hospital had kept Gene for a little longer than they would have normally kept someone who had received a kidney transplant. After the transplant, there were some complications with anemia and a few other issues with pneumonia. The actual operation went extremely well and his body appeared to accept the kidney without reservation.

"When can we go?" Kelli asked.

"They said today. It should be any time, as soon as the doctor releases him," I said.

Gene was already dressed in his khaki pants, shirt and shoes. He had his bed made when we showed up and was sitting in the chair watching the news. The month or more that he had been in the hospital was more than he could process, now that he was able to process again.

"Well, fuck. Kelli, go get shit head and I a cup of cafeteria coffee," Gene said.

Kelli shook her head as she looked at her father. He was on the edge of the bed doing half-assed sit-ups.

"I will if you'll sit in the chair and sit still," she said.

"Fine," he said as he sat up in the bed.

"Ok, anything else?" she asked.

"Not for me. Gene?" I asked.

"Coffee, baby. That's all," he said.

"Wait a minute, can you even *have* coffee?" I asked.

"I can *have* whatever I can lift to my mouth. When I get home I'll have a fucking scotch. You think you're big enough to stop me from drinking a coffee, shit head? I still know a few things about whipping the ass of a snot-nosed kid," he said.

"Get him a coffee," I said, pointing to the door.

Kelli walked toward the door and laughed as she gave me a kiss. After she stepped through the door, Gene looked at me and smiled.

"You know I'm toying with you, don't ya son?" he asked.

"I do," I responded as I sat down in the chair by the door.

"Well, I sold the dealership. I wanted you to know. While I've been in here, the general manager finished the deal. It's done. I have a few things to sign, but it's gone," he said smiling.

"Oh, shit. You sure that's what you want to do, especially now?" I asked.

"Well, I fucking did it, didn't I?" he responded.

He sure had a way with words.

"I suppose you did. Well, what are you going to do now?" I asked.

"I have a few ideas. Retire. I was going to anyway. Kelli doesn't need to run that dealership. Hell, I haven't told her yet, but I will. Same as before, keep your fucking yap shut, got me?" he said.

"Mums the word, Gene," I said as I motioned my fingers across my lips as if I were zipping them shut.

"Smart-ass," he said.

I smiled.

"So, you're never going to find out who donated the kidney are you?" I asked.

"No, they said they had some form of record, but the name isn't published or something. He donated it and left. Sounded like he was on *a* list, or on *my* list or something for a while. I don't remember what all they told me. Son-of-a-bitch told them they could tell me it was from Santa Claus or the Pied Piper or some smart-ass thing. Doctor said he actually said that – the donor. The Pied fucking Piper. I don't remember what all they said I was still loopy from the anesthesia. I did ask the other day if I could donate money to his family, and they said no," he said, shaking his head in disbelief.

"Well, the important thing is that you're in good health. He'll be rewarded for his gift to you ten-fold," I said.

"I believe that," Gene said as he stood from his chair.

Kelli walked through the door with two cups of coffee and a bottle of juice. Gene gave me the nastiest stink eye he could manage and pursed his lips as she walked in.

"Here you two go. Are you getting along better?" she asked as she handed each our cups of coffee.

Gene shook his head.

"He's stubborn, Kelli," I said.

"You're telling me," she laughed as she handed him his coffee.

Oddly, sitting in the room with Kelli and Gene, I felt as if we were a family. His arguing and his stubborn nature were his own way of accepting me into his life. I felt for the first time in as long as I could remember that I was a part of something bigger than myself.

With the upcoming holidays, I felt as if I would be filled with a different, welcomed, and newfound love. I smiled at Kelli as she sat on my lap.

"She used to sit on my lap like that when she was little. I'd bounce my knee up and down. Hell, half the time, she'd fall off. She'd always get back on, though. She's as stubborn as I am," he laughed.

"You're telling me," I laughed.

SCOTT

The door opened and the doctor walked in. I patted Kelli on the leg and motioned for her to stand so I could stand up and address the doctor.

"Mr. Parks are you ready to go home?" the doctor asked.

"God damned straight, doc," Gene said as he stood from his chair.

"Daddy!" Kelli said.

"Well, I am. Shit, I been in this son-of-a-bitch for a month. I'm ready to get the fuck out. I've got shit to take care of. Sorry doc," he said.

"Well, I've signed you out. You're ready to go," the doctor said.

I turned to the doctor and motioned for the door.

"Oh no you don't. You two pricks are in cahoots with each other. Couple of fucking doctors going to go out in the hallway and plot and plan," Gene said loudly.

"Daddy!" Kelli said.

"Well, it's the truth. Get that ape on a leash," he said.

"Fine, Gene," I looked at the doctor and rolled my eyes.

"So, are there any special instructions we need to follow," I asked.

"The basics. He's actually in good health. He's finishing an antibiotic for his pneumonia, not the kidney. He has three scripts and the iron. One is for the kidney, to assist in that his body doesn't reject it, the antibiotic, and pain medication. He needs to rest. Drink fluids. Eat plenty of fiber, and see his doctor in two weeks for a check-up. That's it. He's extremely fortunate," he said.

"So…" I couldn't think of anything else to say.

"So, I can leave now, you big ape. Come on Kelli, these two can stay and swap spit all they want," Gene said.

"Daddy!" Kelli said.

The doctor laughed. I couldn't help but laugh. Gene approached my right side as I faced the door.

"You staying or coming with us?" he asked.

"I'm driving," I said.

"Thank you doctor," I said as I extended my hand.

As he shook my hand, the reality set in that we were actually leaving. It had become so common for Kelli and I to come here to visit, I felt as if this was going to become a normal occurrence. With great relief I walked through the door and to the elevator as Kelli and Gene walked hand-in-hand.

As we walked to the car, I sighed. Again, overcome with the relief that we were leaving this place. I never really cared much for hospitals. Probably yet another reason I don't practice.

"It's right here," I said as I pointed to the car.

As soon as we approached it, I realized Gene had snuck out of the hospital without the assistance of a wheelchair. This ornery bastard

118

was going to be a handful. I smiled and laughed a little thinking of his antics and smart mouthed attitude.

"Gene, you made it out of there without a wheelchair, good job," I said as we walked up to the rear of the car.

"I'm full of tricks. Toss me your keys and I'll show you how to drive this god damned thing. Hell, I'll blow the cobs out of it for ya," he said.

I looked him in the eye as he held out his hand. He was dead serious.

"Well?" he asked.

"Daddy?" Kelli said.

"Hell, I've sold more of these damned things than he'll ever own in ten lifetimes," he said to Kelli.

I thought of him selling the dealership and the fact that he may never get to drive a car like this again. Considering the nature of the car, the dealer may not have another for a year or so. Regardless of his desire to drive, or my desire to let him, it wasn't quite that simple.

I cannot ride in a car with someone unless I truly trust them. It's a character defect of mine. Relinquishing that control, for me, is impossible - unless there is trust.

Total trust.

"Shotgun," I screamed as I tossed him the keys.

Chapter Twenty

*E*RIK. "Ask me, it's a good fuckin' deal, Doc. Hell, she probably didn't wanna run that damned place anyway. Shit, Kelli runnin' a BMW dealer? That's just ridiculous. Her ability to sell is not her most prepossessing quality," Teddy said.

"Jesus, Crash," I said, making note of his newfound vocabulary.

"Well, it's something she'd have to work on," he said.

"Train, grab that waitress when you get a minute. Hell, I'm parched," Teddy said as he finished his beer.

"Got it, Crash," A-Train said.

"So, what you all gonna do for the holidays?" Teddy asked.

"Well, Kelli and I are cooking, Gene's coming to our house for Thanksgiving," I responded.

"How's that set with ya, Doc?" he asked.

"Real well, Crash. Real well. Shit, I never would have guessed I'd be where I am today, *ever*. I'm here, though. Hell, I like it. I like it a lot," I admitted.

"Yeah, won't be long, and we won't be able to sit out here anymore," Teddy said, motioning to the patio seating.

"When you gonna get your bagger, Doc?" Train asked.

"I don't know, before spring. If I wait too long, they'll be out of the 2013's, and that 2014 looks like shit in my opinion," I responded.

"That fairing has a hole in the middle of it. Looks fuckin' retarded," Teddy said.

"I agree," I said.

"Well, if you need a ride to Tulsa, let me know. I'll haul ya down," A-Train offered.

"Appreciate it, Train," I said.

"This getting dark early is horseshit, you ask me. Every year it gets dark earlier. Where's my fucking beer, Train?" Teddy said as he looked to the west.

"It gets dark the same time every year, Crash. Jesus. You're just getting old," I laughed.

"Kiss my ass, Doc. Still take your ass any day," Teddy bragged.

"I got a twenty on Doc," A-Train said.

"Shit, Train, I got a hundred pounds on this little prick," Teddy said as he motioned my direction.

"Yeah, but Doc's fast as fuck," A-Train said as he took a drag off his cigarette.

"Well, I ain't plannin' on boxin' his dumb ass. I'm just gonna beat him like a red headed step child," Teddy replied.

"There's the rabbit," A-Train said, pointing to truck driving into the parking lot.

"What's he doing driving a cage?" I laughed.

"Dumped a rental in Vermont or wherever the fuck he went. Hit sand when some shit-bird pulled out in front of him. Fucked up his knee and hip. Not bad. That hard-tail kills his back," A-Train answered.

I looked at Teddy. Teddy shrugged his shoulders. Bunny parked his truck and started walking across the lot.

"Hell, he looks fine to me," I said.

"I don't think he's hurt bad, just fucked up his hip a little. It doesn't hurt him to walk, just to ride," A-Train said.

"I ain't dumped one yet," Teddy said as he knocked on the wooden table.

"No, but your drunken ass knocked over about two dozen when I was in Afghanistan," A-Train laughed.

"Well, that ain't dumping one," Teddy snarled, "And where's that fuckin' waitress?"

"I'll get her as soon as Bunny gets here," A-Train said.

"So Bunny, you dumped one on your little vacation?" I asked as he walked up to the table.

I shook his hand and hugged him as he tossed his keys on the table. He winced when I hugged him.

"Damn, you alright?" I asked.

"Yeah, just fucked up my hip. Knee is a little banged up. Just hurts when I twist wrong. Doc said a few weeks and I'll be fine," he said.

"What ya want to drink?" A-Train asked.

"Water," Easter answered.

"Water? Since when do you drink water?" Teddy asked.

"Since I'm on pain killers for this hip," he answered.

"Well, get me two of them big beers. And a plate of them fried pickles," Teddy said.

Baby Girl III

I shook my head at Teddy. Some of the things that he eats surprised me. I know that not everyone is as health conscious as I am, but his choices in food make me laugh sometimes. I never eat fried food, and rarely eat anything that isn't considered healthy.

"Fried pickles?" I asked, still shaking my head.

"Ever ate one?" Teddy asked, leaning his stool back onto the rear legs.

I shook my head, "No. I wouldn't eat one if I had to."

"Maybe that's part of your problem, Doc. Live a little. Try new shit, it's the little things that can help make ya a new degree of happy," Teddy said.

"Hell, I've tried em. They're damned good," A-Train said as he walked toward the entrance to the bar.

"Me too, they're good. Get a *couple* plates of 'em," Easter said in A-Train's direction.

"Fryin' a pickle ain't something that a guy would ever decide to do on his own, but I'm glad someone decided to fry one up. You suppose they got a guy somewhere that just tries new shit, and decides if it's good or not?" Teddy asked.

"What the hell are you talking about?" I asked.

Teddy rocked his stool onto all four legs, and leaned forward. He rested his forearms onto the table. He rubbed his beard and appeared to go deep into thought. He looked at Bunny and glanced back in my direction. I raised my hands into the air to encourage him to speak.

"What, Crash? *Say it*. What's on your mind?" I asked.

"Well, I was thinkin'. Like a fried Oreo cookie. Or them bananas at the state fair. The ones dipped in chocolate and nuts and shit. And them mountain oysters. You know, fried cows nuts. Who decides to cook up this shit? I wonder about these things sometimes. Actually I wonder about them a lot. You think the food and drug administration has a team of fellas that just sit in a lab and cook shit? Maybe another team of tasters? They hand 'em a fried banana dipped in fish batter or something. And the guy says, *Oh fuck. Goddamn. That tastes like shit. Dip that fucker in chocolate.* So the cooker, you know the brains behind the operation...he says, *Oh shit, my bad. Okay.* Comes back in half an hour. Hands the fella a banana dipped in chocolate. Then the guy says, *Add some crushed peanuts, and we got us a deal.* You think that's how they do it?" he looked at Easter and then back at me.

"Are you fuckin serious?" I asked.

Bunny was laughing semi-hysterically.

"I ain't fuckin' around. Twenty years ago, you couldn't go in a restaurant and get fried pickles. Not here, or anywhere for that matter. Now, you can't swing a dead cat in this town without runnin' into a joint that sells 'em. Who in the fuck decided to release 'em to the public?" Teddy asked, waving his arms frantically.

A-Train walked toward the table with two beers and two glasses of water.

"I miss the joke of the day?" he asked as he started setting the glasses down in front of us.

"Crash wants to know who invented fried pickles. He thinks there's government involvement," Easter laughed.

"You fucking serious?" A-Train asked as he placed a beer in front of Teddy.

I nodded.

"Well, tell me Mr. Marine. Who the fuck invents this shit? Fried pickles? Couldn't get 'em when we were kids, now everyone sells 'em," Teddy said, waving his arms in a circle again.

A-Train started laughing and slapped Easter on the shoulder.

"God damn, Train. My fucking hip, go easy on me," Easter complained as he arched his back slowly.

"Shit, Bun. Sorry. What do you think people would think if they thought four bikers were sitting here trying to decide who invented fried pickles?" A-Train asked.

The waitress walked out with two plates of pickles.

"Here you fellas go, fried pickles. Anything else I can get you?" the waitress said as she placed the two plates of pickles onto the table.

"Napkins," Teddy said as he leaned forward and grabbed a handful of pickles.

She reached into her apron and pulled out four sets of silverware wrapped in cloth napkins. She set them on the table.

"Anything else?" she asked.

"Who invented these things?" Easter asked.

She turned and looked at Bunny, placing her hands on her hips.

"*What's that*, Bunny?" she said, leaning forward and looking at the name on the front of his vest.

"Fried pickles. Who invented them?" he asked.

She turned and looked at each of us, and back toward Bunny.

"Seriously?" she asked.

Bunny nodded.

"I don't know. George Washington Carver invented peanut butter. He was a scientist," she said.

"Yeah, see? I told ya. It ain't just some random shit we're eatin'. Someone's inventing this, someone *big*," Teddy said as he grabbed a few more pickles from the plate.

"Well, it isn't Carver, he's dead," she said as she turned to walk away.

"Big things and little things, fellas. Life's full of each. The big things settle themselves, they're a given. They're the easy ones. The small things, they're the fuckin' toughest. They're left up for interpretation," Teddy said as he grabbed another pickle and bit it in two.

Baby Girl III

He took a drink of beer.

"It's the small things, the *little fuckers* that matter. We all stay worried about the big things, and we can't change 'em. The big ones are the way they are. We need to focus more on the small things to make life worth livin'. The details. Have a pickle fellas," Teddy said as he stuck his finger in his beer and nodded his head toward the two plates of pickles.

I thought about what he had said. The big things and the little things. The details are what matters. Teddy was simple, but he had a good point.

A-Train and Easter each grabbed a handful of pickles.

The small things.

Fuck it.

I reached in and grabbed a handful of pickles.

Chapter Twenty-One

*K*ELLI. Most people are of the opinion that we are an extension of our parents. One more generation of the thoughts, beliefs, and morale values instilled upon us from the manner that we were raised by them. I believe that. My father was instrumental in the development of the person that I had become.

I am the person that I am today because of how my father raised me. He explained to me how life would be, what I should pay attention to, and the manner in which I should treat other people. For the most part, he was correct in all respects.

Erik has helped me understand that my sexual choices I have made as an adult were decided long before I consciously made them. My sexual desires, what I like and don't like - sexually speaking, were decided subconsciously long before I was even ten years old.

My father did a good job of raising me. I have always thought no one could or would love me as much as my father.

Until I met Erik.

Our parents love us because we are their children. It isn't that they don't have a choice, but they sure don't have much of one. They love us unconditionally because we are a product of them, an extension of them, and a living part of each of them.

When someone other than our parents loves us - truly loves us - it is a different love. Not better or more meaningful, but different. Erik's love for me made me feel as if every day with him was a gift. A gift of the love that I never believed even existed. I still woke up every morning and expected it all to be a dream.

We don't always immediately realize that there is anything wrong in or with our lives until someone comes along and makes it right.

SCOTT

That one person that completes our life - and makes it all seem right - allows us to see how wrong it was before they came along.

Without that person entering our life, we may live forever with thoughts that everything is perfect. We don't have anything to compare it to until they come along. Once we're exposed to them, and have the knowledge of what it is that they provide us, we can't ever be satisfied without them.

Because they, and only they, make what is an otherwise dull meaningless life vibrant and full of passion.

Erik said he would ruin me.

He certainly did that.

As a young child, we believe a dandelion is beautiful. Until we see a rose for the first time. Once exposed to the rose, a dandelion no longer is the expression of beauty it once was. The rose ruined it for us. Now, the rose has established beauty in our mind, and is our means of measuring magnificence.

Erik was my rose.

"Well, I must say that meal was specfuckingtacular. Where'd you learn to cook, son?" daddy asked.

"I watched some videos online," Erik said from the kitchen, laughing.

Daddy leaned back into the couch and relaxed. I sat down across the room from him in the loveseat. Erik carried in a tray with coffee, cream, and sugar.

"Here we go," he said as he set it down on the coffee table in front of the couch.

"Well, wherever you learned to cook, you did a good job - both of you. That was the best Thanksgiving dinner I've ever had. I appreciate it. Today, I am grateful for the two of you having each other," he said as he took a drink from his coffee cup.

"Thank you. Kelli worked as hard as I did," Erik said as he sat at the other end of the couch from daddy.

"Well, either way, I enjoyed it, thank you," daddy said, glancing back and forth between Erik and I.

Erik nodded as he took a sip from his cup.

"Thank you daddy," I said.

It was exciting to me to have Thanksgiving dinner at our house. It was always something I wondered if I would *ever* do, having my father come to *my* house for a holiday meal. Until I moved in with Erik, I never expected to have a desire to have any form of holiday celebration at my house. Doing so made me both nervous and excited. Now that it was over, it was very rewarding to have done so. I felt, for once in my life, like a true adult.

"Well, I have an announcement, if you want to call it that. It has nothing to do with the great meal; it's just something that I decided to do," Daddy said.

"Okay, what is it?" I said, excited for what the *announcement* might be.

Erik nodded.

"You paying attention, shit head?" Daddy laughed.

"Yes sir," Erik chuckled as he crossed his legs and sat back on the couch.

"Well, as you both now know, I sold the dealership. The deal's done. Under contract, I stay thirty days with the new owner for some formalities, and work two days a week. But, the deal is done, and it's over. So," he took a deep breath, sat up on the edge of the couch and exhaled.

"I bought the Harley dealership," he smiled and looked back and forth between Erik and I as he spoke.

"Daddy, really?" I asked, not quite believing he wasn't going to retire.

"Gene, I thought you were going to retire?" Erik asked.

Daddy smiled and leaned back into the couch. He took a sip from his cup and looked at Erik.

"Son, I bought it for you two. Kelli doesn't need to run a BMW dealership. That was my dream, not hers. The guy that owned that place was an asshole. I got him down to a manageable price, so I bought it. We should take possession in about three weeks. I don't want you two to run it, I want to give it to you, as a gift," he said as he nodded his head toward Erik.

"Daddy? What?" I couldn't believe what he was saying.

"Well, maybe now you can give this ape a good deal on that bike he wants," he laughed as he slapped Erik on the shoulder.

"Gene, I don't even know what to..." Erik didn't finish before daddy interrupted.

"Son, just keep your gob shut. I don't need sentiment. I don't need tears or a thank you. You both knew I intended on giving the BMW dealership to Kelli. My being sick and some soul searching made me change that. So, I'm giving this to you two, and it actually saves me some money. I can put my extra in a trust," he said as he handed Erik his coffee cup.

"Get me another cup of coffee, son. Make yourself useful," he said.

Erik took the cup and walked into the kitchen.

"Daddy, are you serious?" I asked.

"Yes, it's already done, baby. It's the least I can do. It'll let you two make your own business. You can hire whoever you want to run it, do service work, sell bikes, whatever you want. You can develop it, build it, and watch it grow. Just like I did with the BMW dealership," he said.

Erik walked back into the room with a carafe of coffee and daddy's coffee cup.

"Sir, I don't even know what to say, it's overwhelming to be quite honest," Erik said as he handed daddy his cup of coffee.

"Well, get over it, I did."

"Daddy was just saying that it would be our own dealership and we get to decide who works for us and everything, Erik," I said as I looked up at Erik.

Erik shook his head and looked at daddy as he sat down.

"I'm too excited, I have to pee," I said as I stood up to go to the bathroom.

This was just too much to process. I walked to the bathroom overwhelmed. Erik and I owning the only Harley-Davidson dealership in the largest city in Kansas was almost too much to believe. Having Erik own a Harley dealer would be like having a wolf in charge of the chicken coop. I washed my hands and laughed an excited laugh. I looked into the mirror and smiled.

The girl looking back at me made me proud. She was no longer a girl - she was growing into a woman. I dried my hands and turned back toward the living room. As I walked into the living room, Erik and daddy were sitting right next to each other whispering. When I walked in, they immediately stopped talking.

"What are you two telling secrets about?" I asked.

Erik had an odd smile on his face, and was shaking his head slowly. Daddy looked puzzled.

"It's nothing important baby. Just man talk, no worries," daddy said as he scooted back to his side of the couch.

Erik looked at me and smiled a funny smile.

I looked at daddy and back at Erik. I shook my head and smiled.

And I sat down in between the man that raised his little girl and the one that made me a feel like the most beautiful woman in the world.

Chapter Twenty-Two

*E*RIK. "You're serious?"
"Dead serious. Kelli and I already talked about it," I said.
"Holy shit, brother. That's a dream come true. Son-of-a-bitch. You have any idea what that means to me? Any at all?" The Bone said as he hugged me.

"I have an *idea*," I said as I pulled myself away and patted him on the back.

"Shit, running the repair shop? Fuck, Doc, I'll have that place making you two some serious money. And we won't be building hi-performance bikes and turning customers away when the motor blows up, either," he said.

"They better not be blowing up, or Kelli will fire your ass," I laughed.

"Don't worry about that, Doc. I'll make the two of you damned proud. Hell, this is all I ever needed, a good shop and some store front. God damn, this is exciting," he said as he rubbed his hands together.

"Yeah, it's kind of overwhelming, to be quite honest with you. I've never really had a job. Shit this is all new to me," I chuckled.

"Hell, the owner never does anything. Just goes on vacations, huh Doc?" The Bone laughed.

It was nice seeing Derek this excited. He was a damned good man with a tremendous amount of talent. To see him have the ability and the resources to make a shop his own would be nice. I crossed my arms knowing that he would not let Kelli or I down. If I had the ability to hire anyone to run the repair shop, Derek would be my first choice.

"Well, they're all waiting for us to tell them what's up, you ready?" he asked.

"I am if you are," I said as I grabbed the handle to his office door.

We both stepped through the office door and into the shop of waiting brethren.

"Get yer ass chewed?" Teddy asked as I walked out into the shop.

"Yeah, he's a mean son-of-a-bitch," I laughed.

The Bone stepped out into the shop beside me and put his arm around my shoulder. He squeezed my upper arm in his massive hand and pulled me into his shoulder.

"Alright fellas. Doc here has an announcement. I need you all to keep your fucking mouths shut and listen up. This is a biggie. This club will see the rewards of this for a long fucking time. Doc, the floor is yours," he said as he let loose of my arm and slapped me on the back.

"Well, as you all know, Kelli's dad is out of the hospital, doing really well, and he has sold the BMW dealership," I took a breath.

Everyone began to clap.

"God damn it, fellas. That ain't it. I told you to shut the fuck up," The Bone screamed, barely able to contain his excitement.

All eyes were on me. I looked down at the floor and back up to the crowd. About twenty of the closest knit members were in attendance.

"Well hell. I don't even know how to say this. To tell you the truth, I'm still having a hard time believing it," I took another deep breath.

"Kelli's father bought the Harley dealer. And he gave it to Kelli and I as a gift. We own the fucking Harley dealership, fellas. Kelli and I," I shouted.

"Holy shit Doc. Now you can get that Glide you been eye ballin'." A-Train screamed.

"You fuckin' serious, Doc?" Teddy asked as he walked up beside me.

I nodded.

"Sum bitch, congratulations, Doc. Who's gonna run her for ya?" he asked.

Everyone started walking toward The Bone and I, talking and shouting as they approached. It appeared that I wasn't the only one that was excited about the new ownership.

"Haven't decided. Bone's gonna run the shop, I know that," I said.

"Well, that's a no brainer," Teddy laughed as he slapped Bone on the back.

"When you gonna take it over?" Teddy asked.

"Probably here in a few weeks, maybe two," I answered.

Several members came up and shook my hand and gave the

congratulatory slap on the back. I felt like some form of celebrity at a fundraiser.

Teddy, Shaky, A-Train and Jake all gathered around the Bone and I, and everyone was attempting to talk at once. All of the commotion added to the excitement of everything. My excitement was something that I wasn't or hadn't yet become used to.

As a child, I would get excited for Christmas to come. As it approached sometimes my excitement would be so overwhelming that I would make myself sick. When Christmas got within a week of arrival, I was never convinced I would make it that far, or that for some reason it would be cancelled or never actually happen.

As I got older, the excitement diminished. By the time I was ten, I was not excited about Christmas any longer; at least not as excited as I was as a toddler or young child. I became more concerned with today and far less concerned with what tomorrow may bring. As I began to be concerned only with what today involved and offered, my life changed. Ten or eleven years old for me became a turning point in my life. My performance in school had become more important, and I began getting perfect grades.

I attributed my good grades to my focus on today, and I made a conscious effort to become focused on today, and never focus on tomorrow. I stopped looking at the future for anything that it may offer me. In retrospect, this may have been the beginning of a life of not being able to be in a meaningful relationship.

I was no longer concerned with what tomorrow could or would bring, because tomorrow may never arrive. I lived in the today. I lived for what was in front of me, and not what may be in the future. I maintained this posture, or this belief, throughout the remaining portion of my life. It was easy, it was accurate, and it proved to be less stressful.

Recently, and certainly after falling in love with Kelli, this changed. Every day seemed to bring more change, and more invitation to look at or into the future. Tomorrow holds promise, hope, and excitement. Now, I often find myself looking at what tomorrow *may* bring. I think of what I may need to change in me or my manner of doing things that would make our future a better life for both of us. I found now that I had allowed myself to become excited again for what the future may hold.

"Fellas, I'm excited about this. I feel like I may just vomit," I laughed as I put my hands on my thighs.

"Aww shit, don't puke, Doc," Teddy laughed.

Everyone shared a laugh and stepped back a little bit.

"Well, it'll be good for *all of us*. Give us all something to do and look forward to and such, huh?" Shakey said.

"I'm sure hoping so, Shakey," I said.

"Where's the Rabbit?" I asked, looking around the shop for Bunny.

"He's over there," A-Train said, pointing to the office.

Bunny was leaning on the wall of the office watching us and smiling. A few others were standing close to him talking.

"Alright fellas, let's go to the bar and celebrate. I'm going to talk to Bunny about some home repairs, I'll meet you out front," I said as I stepped back out of the circle of men.

"Line 'em up fellas, we're headed to Peaks to celebrate!" Bone screamed.

Everyone began hollering and whistling and walking for the entrance of the shop. I walked toward Bunny, who was still leaning on the wall of the office.

"So Bun, is your back still bothering you?" I asked.

"Hip, it was my hip," he responded.

"Hip, hell, I was thinking it was your back. So, is it better?" I asked.

"Yeah, all healed up. I'm good to go. I rode the sled today," he said.

"Well, glad you're better. That's all that matters. That's something else about Gene, huh? Getting the kidney and giving the dealership to Kelli and I?" I asked.

Bunny nodded slowly.

"Takes a pretty selfless person to do that. You know, to just walk into a hospital and say, *I'm going to donate a kidney to a man I don't know*. And you know, *I'm willing to live the rest of my life the way he has lived his, in fear of only having only one kidney*. And then, living a life hoping nothing ever happens," I said.

Bunny nodded, "What you mean, selfless, Doc?"

"You know, not concerned with his self. Doing something just the opposite of selfish," I responded.

"Yeah, I suppose," he said as he pushed himself off of the wall and began to step forward.

This was a perfect time for me to do it. I had to act fast and move faster. I wanted to surprise him as much as I could and try not to get in an argument about it, but I had to *know*.

As quickly as I could, as he stepped past me, I grasped the bottom of his shirt and yanked it up, focusing on his lower torso.

And there it was.

A fresh purple scar.

"What the fuck you doing, Doc?" he said as he yanked himself away from me, pulling his shirt from my grasp.

"Hold up, Bun. We need to talk," I said.

Bunny looked worried. *Genuinely worried.*

"How'd you know, Doc? I don't want anyone knowing. Not Kelli,

Baby Girl III

not him, not the fellas. It's important to me," he stuttered, his voice full of emotion.

He leaned back onto the office wall.

"Bun, it'll stay here. Between you and I," I promised as I extended my hand in his direction.

He shook my hand and tried unsuccessfully to smile.

"But, how'd you know?" he asked.

"Well. The hospital said it was an anonymous donor. When Gene was in recovery, he wanted to know who gave it to him. They doctor on the team responded that, to the best of Gene's recollection, was the Pied Piper, Batman, Superman, or Santa Claus. Hell he couldn't remember. The other day, we had Thanksgiving dinner. Kelli went to the bathroom, and he started talking to me about the dealership, holidays, and the future. I said the word *Easter*," I paused, recalling the look on Gene's face when I said it.

"When I did, he said, *Easter Bunny*. Hell, I thought he was going insane, blurting it out like that. Then, he said, *I just remembered who donated the kidney. The Easter Bunny. That's what the doctor's said.* I probably turned white as a ghost. He went on to telling his story and never gave it another thought. I thought about it, you needing to go out of town, and the bad hip when you returned. Hell, it all began to make sense," I said.

He looked at the floor the entire time I spoke.

"You alright, Bun?" I asked.

He looked up and nodded slowly. His eyes were swollen. He wasn't crying, but he was close.

"You fuckers comin'" Bone screamed into the shop door.

"Yeah, we'll be there in a minute, give us a few," I screamed over my shoulder.

"Bun?" I asked again.

"You remember my pop, Doc?" he asked.

I nodded, recalling the death of Bunny's father. He was a Navy SEAL in Somalia in the early 1990's. Many people claimed to be a SEAL, or wanted to be, but Bunny's father was. And he died attempting to remove a savage from a position of authority in Somalia.

"He died in Somalia. 1993. He was Navy. It ain't about the Navy, but that helped. It's about having a father. You ain't got one. Hell, you finally found the love of your life, and she ain't got a mom. She's only got a father. Between ya, you got one father. Just one. And it seems as he's accepted you, and accepted us. Hell, look at what he did for A-Train. And hell he never met him," he paused and rubbed his eyes.

"I can't change what happened to my pop. Don't want to. Actually, I'm proud he was shot and killed. It makes me remember each day that he was fighting for a free country. I'm proud of him. My pop

135

and people like my pop are the reason we get to get on our scoots and ride to the bar here in a minute. They fight to keep the rest of us free," he looked back down at the floor and kicked the toe of his boot in the dirt.

"I knew my blood type the day of the meeting. But I'll be damned if I want these fellas to know what I did - or anyone for that matter. I don't want or need praise or bullshit like that. I just wanted to do for you and Kelli what I could, Doc. He was a Navy man, A-Train told me. I needed a few days to think, and to pray," he rubbed his legs and took a breath.

"So I told 'em. I said I'd donate it if I had to. If he was actually dying, I'd give it, but only if it came down to it. I said if someone else donated, fine. If dialysis kept him alive, fine. But, I said if he's dying, call me," he rubbed his eyes again.

"And when they called," his voice started cracking.

"Hell..."

"I couldn't get there, Doc..." he held his index finger in the air.

"...I couldn't get there fast enough. It excited me to be able to give this to him, to you, and to Kelli. C'mon, they're gonna leave us," he said as he wiped his eyes.

"So, why tell them the Easter Bunny donated it?" I asked.

"Well, fuck. I don't know. They kept asking if I wanted to leave a note, anything, something for the recipient. They said he'd be extremely grateful. I said, *Tell him the Easter Bunny donated it.* It just came out. I never figured they'd say shit. Guess I was wrong," he said, shaking his head side to side.

"Take care of those that take care of us," I said.

"What's that?" he said.

"You said that when you left our place that day," I said as I put my arm around his shoulder.

"Amen," he said, and we turned to walk out of the shop.

Chapter Twenty-Three

KELLI. "So this weekend we get the keys. Are you excited?" I asked.

"Baby girl, you know I'm excited. It's all we've been talking about for weeks," he responded.

"I'm excited too. Nervous, but excited," I said.

Erik had been acting funny for about a week. Since we bought the house, we had been together every moment of every day for the most part. Spending time with Erik made me so happy. He has taught me so much about myself. I know now who I am, what I have been hiding from my entire life, and why I am the way I am.

I know I am not broken, and that there's nothing wrong with me. I know that Erik is what I need to make my life complete, and I see that every day that we are together. When I need to be, Erik will scold me. When I do well, he always praises me. He tells me I am beautiful, that he is proud of me, and that I am a good girl.

I'm sure to some people, these things would seem meaningless, or ridiculous, but to me they were important. Erik telling me I was a good girl made me happier than almost any gift he could give me. Erik telling me he was proud of me was better than receiving anything I had ever received from anyone else in the past. Being told by Erik that he was proud was better than any material object anyone could ever offer.

Erik didn't tell me he was proud or that I was a good girl just to say it. He said it because he meant it. And, because he meant it, it meant something to me. Erik being proud of me created a desire to continue to make him so.

That desire filled me, and that passion made him proud.

When he said it, I was putty in his hands. I suppose, all things considered, he told me these things for his benefit as well. All I know is that I never want to disappoint Erik. I never want him to stop being proud, and I never want him to stop telling me.

Erik took a drink of his coffee and looked out at the street. His hands were sexy. I liked watching him do things with his hands. His hands made me wet. Hell, everything about Erik made me wet.

"Christmas is right around the corner. What do you want for Christmas, baby girl?" he asked as he turned to face me.

"You," I responded, smiling.

"Your eyes are beautiful, Kelli," he said.

"Thank you," I said as I flipped my hair over my shoulder.

Erik said he likes it when my hair isn't in my face. He said he likes seeing my face, my neck and my ears. He said the more he can see, the more he loves seeing it.

"Seriously, what?" he asked as he finished his coffee.

"You, that's all," I said, nodding my head.

"You have me," he responded.

"That's all I want. You. Forever. You make me smile," I said.

"You make me smile too," he said.

Warren was leaning on the espresso machine watching us talk.

"Did you get your machine fixed, Warren?" I asked.

"All fixed now Kelli, it's good to go," he said as he smiled and tapped the top of the machine.

Erik pulled the lid off of a cup of water and took a drink. He never liked drinking cold things through a straw, and he always removed the lids from them. I liked drinking through straws. Straws made drinking fun.

I took a drink of my coffee and wiped the coffee from my teeth.

"Do you think coffee makes your teeth brown?" I asked Erik.

"Well, if you soaked them in it, I'm sure it would," Erik laughed.

"But not just drinking it?" I asked, wondering if my teeth would eventually be brown from drinking the chai latte.

"Baby, not if you brush them. I don't know, I don't think so," he laughed.

I smiled and drank the rest of my coffee. Something shifted in the cup as I tipped it up. I squinted and looked at Erik as he watched me take the drink.

Warren and his tricks.

I pulled the lid from the cup to see what Warren put inside. He loves to play jokes on everyone that comes in the store. He loves living life, and he always has fun doing it. I set the lid on the table and looked inside the cup.

My heart stopped. It didn't skip. It stopped beating.

Completely.

I looked at Erik.

Baby Girl III

I looked in the cup. My hand started shaking.

"Erik?" I needed to say so much more.

"Baby girl?" Erik said, "Are you okay?"

"Baby girl," he said again.

My head started spinning inside. I couldn't focus on anything. I think for a minute, I was in shock.

I looked at Warren. He covered his mouth with his hand. I looked back at Erik, and into the cup.

"Baby girl?" Erik said, "Are you okay?"

I grasped the cup in my hand and stared. My entire body shook. I lifted my other hand from my lap and held it in front of me. It shook uncontrollably.

He reached for the cup. I let him take it from my grasp as I watched his eyes. Without looking, he dumped the cup into his hand. He turned his hand over and dumped it into the glass of water that was on the table.

And then, for the first time, Erik made me cry like a baby.

He reached toward the center of the table with his left hand, and turned his palm up. I laid my left hand into his and looked into his eyes.

And I began to cry.

He reached into the cup with his right hand. I couldn't watch. I looked into his eyes and cried softly.

"Kelli, I can call you *baby girl*, I can call you *Kelli*, or maybe even *my good little girl*. I can call you my *girlfriend*, or my *good little slut*," he chuckled as his eyes swelled with tears.

"But the one thing I *can't* call you, and I desperately yearn to…" he paused.

"Is my *wife*," he took a short breath and looked directly into my eyes.

"Kelli Parks, will you be my wife?"

I nodded.

He probably expected that. I always nod. I rarely speak. Only lately had I become comfortable speaking around Erik. My submissive nature had always caused me to be quiet around Erik and allow him to do all of the talking. I was always afraid of saying the wrong thing. And now, when I *needed* to say *yes*, all I could do was nod my head.

He slid the ring onto the ring finger of my left hand. The diamond was huge. I have never seen anything more beautiful in my life.

Regardless of who you are, what you believe in, or where you were raised, if you're a girl - you always dream of *one thing*.

A man proposing to you that loves you. And that you love back. I'm sure many women are proposed to that don't accept. I'm sure an equal number are proposed to that *wonder* if the marriage will last – or maybe they *hope*.

But with Erik, I knew.

Knew.

This would be the first and the last time that this would ever happen. This, for both of us, would be forever.

I let the tears fall from my face and looked into his eyes.

"Right now, baby girl, we have each other. But I want more. I know I don't have to prove anything to you. I know I don't. But I want this union, this bond, this marriage of you and I. I want to show you how devoted I am to you. I need you beside me. You allow me to live, to breath, and to survive. I am not afraid to admit it. I want you to be mine for all of what is forever. Again, will you be my wife?" he asked as his wet eyes sparkled.

"I will," I responded.

"I will."

"You, Kelli Parks, just made me more proud than I have ever been," he said.

I nodded.

"Don't worry, your father knows. I went to ask his permission before he got sick, and then I ordered the diamond and had the ring custom made," he said.

"You asked my daddy?" I said, surprised.

"I wanted to do this right, Kelli. I'm only going to do it once, and I wanted to do it as proper as I could," he said as he wiped his eye with his finger.

"Can I ask?" I said.

"What?" he answered.

"What did daddy say?"

"He said he'd be honored to have me be his son. I laughed when he said it, and I corrected him. I said *son-in-law*," Erik paused, looked at the table, and then looked back into my eyes.

"And he said, Don't argue with your father."

Erik shook his head and wiped his eyes again.

"I love you, Kelli," he said as he leaned across the table and kissed me.

"I love you back," I said as our lips parted.

I love you back.

Chapter Twenty-Four

GENE. "Dim the lights, son, it's like fucking daylight in here," I said.

"Where's the dimmer," he asked.

"I know where it is, it's by the office door," Kelli said as she began to walk that direction.

"You need to dim these fucking lights so that god damned ring doesn't blind me," I smiled.

That damned boy has made me so proud. I remember the day I met him. I wasn't too sure about him. He was polite, and he had good posture, I remember that. But he walked a fine line. I know now that he's a fine man. He's confident in who he is, and he doesn't falter. I know one day I will be gone from this earth, and thinking of having him taking care of my Kelli makes me feel better about when I'm going to be gone. I don't think any one man will make her feel more loved, more cared for, and more needed. He praises her as much or more than I ever have.

For that, I am grateful.

"You big dumb fucker, you better learn where shit is around here," I scolded him.

He shook his head and rolled his eyes at me.

"God damn, Erik. This place looks huge. Bigger now than it ever has before. Hell I never really paid attention before," the big boy with the beard said.

"What's your name son," I asked him.

"I'm Teddy. They call me Crash," he said as he leaned toward me and shook my hand.

"You're a big sum bitch, ain't ya?" I asked as I let go of his hand.

"Well, I'm losing weight, down to 250, all muscle. I'm the boyfriend of Kelli's best friend, Heather," he said as he pointed to Heather.

"Well, you're big enough to eat hay and shit in the street," I said as I looked him from head to toe.

"You're the fella that tipped over all the damned bikes, aren't you?" I asked, remembering the story Erik and Kelli told me about the fella names *Crash*.

He nodded and looked at Erik. Erik shrugged his shoulders.

Another one of them walked up and held his hand out. He was a real nice looking fellow, a little taller than Erik. He had a nice sense of presence about him, like he was a man that could be trusted.

"Derek Jackson, sir. They call me The Bone. I'm the president of this mess of a club," he said.

"Pleasure to meet you, Derek. You're running the shop, right?" I asked.

He nodded and smiled from ear to ear.

"Yeah, Erik told me about you. I'm excited for you, son," I said as I shook his hand.

"I won't let you down, sir," he said, standing in front of me looking me in the eyes.

"Well, let's get one thing straight. I'm here tonight for this clusterfuck of a send-off, and this son-of-a-bitch has nothing to do with me. This is Erik and Kelli's. You'll never let me down, because this place isn't mine, and I don't give a fuck about it," I said, laughing.

"Well, I won't let them down," he said as he smiled.

"I imagine not," I responded.

"You must be the *A-Train*," I said as I approached the boy with the short hair.

He stopped walking past us and turned around.

"Yes sir, Alec Jacob," he wiped his hands on his jeans and shook my hand.

"Pleasure is mine, sir," he said.

"I could tell you were a Marine by how you walked, son," I said.

"Once and always, sir," he said.

"I'm glad you're here, son," I said.

"As am I, sir," he responded.

I stood there and began looking around the dealership, making him feel less uneasy about being in my presence. After a moment, he walked away, toward the others.

When I did what I could for Kelli, I did it because *she* asked me to. She explained to me what had happened, or at least what she thought happened. I never met the kid before, but I felt as if I needed to do whatever I could to help him. It was nice to put a face with the name, and to finally see who he was and what he looked like. I could tell from looking into his eyes that he was a good man. He was little war torn maybe, but a good man none-the-less. Meeting him made me happy that I had helped him what little I could. In his eyes, regardless of what *actually* happened, he did nothing wrong.

He walked through the sales floor and looked at the bikes, smiling. These boys were sure proud to be a part of this in either helping Erik and Kelli by working here, or just knowing that the dealership was finally in the hands of someone that would run it in a manner that they found acceptable. Seeing them happy made me happy.

I walked up beside Erik and followed him as he walked through the shop. He looked around, taking in all of what was there, and where things were. A few other boys filtered in as we walked around and admired the facility.

When we walked back into the sales floor, Erik went to talk to Kelli. There were a few people talking by the Harley gear that was beside the sales floor – shirts, and jackets and such. One man was sitting on a motorcycle on the sales floor. He was about as big as Erik, and had similar tattoos and a shaved head. As he grabbed ahold of the handlebars, a tattoo on the back side of his arm caught my eye. I slowly walked up to the right side of him, studying the tattoo as I walked. It wasn't the *tattoo* that caught my eye, it was *what* it depicted.

A Navy anchor.

"You a sailor, son?" I asked as I looked at his tattoo.

"No sir," he said as he moved his arm.

He seemed a little self-conscious about it.

"My father *was*," he said over his right shoulder.

He added emphasis on the word was. I needed to tread lightly.

"I was a sailor. Vietnam. Gunner on a swift boat. They called me *Gunner*. Gunner Parks. My *name* is Gene Parks, I'm Kelli's father," I said in a soft tone.

He studied at me for a long second, and proceeded to speak.

"They called my pop *Bunny*. He was a SEAL. SEAL Team Three. He died in Somalia in 1993. Kid shot him in the throat. He bled out on the way back to the chopper," he said.

"Pleasure to meet you," I said as I extended my hand.

"My name is Steve, sir. Steve Easter. Pleasure sir," he said as he grabbed my hand and gave it a firm shake.

As he shook my hand with his, I felt it tremble. I looked at his vest and saw the name patch on the left side.

Bunny.

The Easter Bunny.

My goddamned heart skipped. I stood, his hand in mine, knowing that this was the man that saved my life. He was the one that gave an old man that he never met another chance at living life. I would have given him anything I had. Hell, I would have given him *everything*.

Yet.

He wanted nothing. He didn't even want recognition. Or praise. I released his hand. There was so much I wanted to say, but I didn't dare. I needed to respect his wishes. He had his reasons for wanting to go unnoticed, whatever they were. To truly appreciate what he did for me, and why, I needed to practice what I always preached.

Never miss a good opportunity to keep your fucking mouth shut.

"Nice to meet you, Steve. I'm sorry about your father. I never had a son, always wanted one. I'll be adopting that dumb fuck over there here pretty soon," I said as I pointed at Erik.

He laughed. As he did, I chuckled.

"I suppose, you all adopted Kelli, so to speak. So, in a sense, I'm adopting all of you. What are you going to do here for Erik and Kelli?"

"Nothing sir, I work construction. Home remodels. Times are tough. I make it from job to job," he said lightly as he looked at the handlebars of the motorcycle.

"Construction? Well, I'll be dipped in shit. I don't know if dumbass or Kelli told you, but I just retired. I need to build a shop onto the side of my house, but I need it to be a damn nice one. What do you know about building garages onto an existing home?" I asked.

"Quite a bit, sir," he responded as his eyes lit up.

"It's going to have to be top-notch, I live out east in one of those high profile neighborhoods," I bragged, smiling.

"I understand fully sir. My work is second to none," he said as he stepped off of the bike and onto the sales floor.

"I'd love to give you a bid," he said as he reached for his rear pocket.

He reached in his pocket and pulled out his wallet. He opened it, removed a crumpled business card, and handed it to me.

"My number is on the card. You give me a call, and I'll give you a bid," he said, smiling from ear to ear.

"Well, the money doesn't matter to me son. I don't need a *bid*. I need the work done. I need it done by a man that's honest, trustworthy, has a high standard for himself, and can make it look like the new addition had been on the house since the beginning. In a perfect world, as I like to say, he'd also be the son of a sailor," I said, smiling.

"I'm that man sir," he said.

"Well, I'll give you a call, we can look at it together and see when you can get started," I said.

"I'll look forward to that call, sir," he said.

He smiled and nodded his head. When he turned to walk away, I reached for my wallet. I opened it and looked at the card before I put it in.

Steve Easter. Honest. Trustworthy. Loyal. On the bottom was his phone number, and in the upper right hand corner, an Easter Bunny.

The Easter Bunny.

Chapter Twenty-Five

*E*RIK. Kelsey Theodore Wilson. Otherwise known as *Teddy*.
My best friend.

He didn't judge, was open-minded, and he wasn't afraid to tell me when I was making a mistake. Friends like him are once in a lifetime, and they're more valuable than gold. I attributed the majority of my progress to several discussions that we had throughout my relationship with Kelli, and the fact that he wasn't afraid to tell me when he thought I was fucking up.

"Un-fucking believable is what it is," he said as he set his mug of beer onto the table.

"Yeah, it's something. Hell, I've always hated change. But right now, to turn back the clock to a year ago? I wouldn't accept it," I said as I looked at into the parking lot.

"So, you used to the heft of it yet?" he asked.

"Hell, Crash. A bike's a bike. Bagger, chopper, they're all the same," I said.

"Well, you got her looking real nice with them apes and those bags. Sounds good with those pipes," he said as he nodded his head.

"Kelli loves it," I said.

"Bet she does. Hell, I'd have to be wanting a ride pretty damned bad to sit on your chopper on a little seat stuck to the fender with a fucking suction cup. That, my friend, is the craziest shit I ever seen. You know, when I was a kid, I had one of them guns that shot them darts with a suction cup on the end. I used to watch cartoons and shoot the T.V.," he paused and chuckled as he took a drink.

"Well, them darts would fall off the T.V. after a second or two. Always wanted 'em to stay there forever, but they wouldn't. I always think of them darts falling off when I'd see Kelli on that seat of yours.

SCOTT

Wondering how much longer it'd be before she just fell off," he laughed.

"So, cruise control, stereo, and a soft seat, you gonna ride that fucker to Arizona bike week?" he asked.

I nodded.

"Taking Kelli?" he asked.

I nodded.

"Yeah, we already talked about it. I'm going, and taking her. I'm headed south when it's over to see my witch friend. Haven't seen her in years," I said.

"Shit, I ain't looking to be around no damned witch. I'm haulin' Heather with me, but fuck that. I'll stay north and wait for you to come back up. Ain't looking to get any spells cast on me," he laughed as he finished his beer.

I laughed.

Trying to explain to people the intricacies of my friend sometimes proved difficult at best. It never changed how I felt about her. She was as good as gold. I'd used the talisman as a crutch through the problems with Kelli's father, and I wanted to tell her how things worked out. Sometimes a face to face talk worked so much better than a phone call or an email.

I looked out at my new bike and smiled.

"You can stare at her all you want, Doc. She ain't gonna change," he laughed.

"Hell, I know. It's new. I like looking at it," I chuckled.

"June's gonna be here before you know it," Teddy said, referring to our wedding date.

"I know it. Hell, I'm ready now," I said.

For so much of my life, I lived it hoping from time-to-time I could turn the clock back and live at a different part of my life. Go back to the past and live it over in a different fashion. Now, I couldn't wait for the tomorrow's to get here. Whatever tomorrow brought for Kelli and I, I wanted it. She truly has changed my life. I have no one but her to thank for how well my life was going now.

For that, I was truly grateful.

"So, when do you think you and Heather will get married?" I asked.

Teddy had his beer mug tipped forward. He had his finger in the glass, feeling the temperature of the beer.

"You ever wonder Doc...well, about them jugs that keep hot things hot and cold things cold?" he asked.

"A thermos?" I asked.

"Yeah, a thermos. How's that sum bitch know whether to keep something hot or keep it cold? This is the kind of shit that makes me sit in bed at night and wonder. Now, me and Heather? Well, I don't know. Now that you and Kelli are getting' hitched, we're talking about it more. I'm ready. Heather does it for me. I like the fact that she's tempestuous. I just want her to be comfortable, and know I ain't doin' it 'cause you did it," he said as he pulled his finger from his beer.

"I don't know about the thermos, Teddy," I lied, shaking my head at the 'new' Teddy.

"As far as you and Heather - I suppose when you're ready, you're ready," I said as I finished my water.

"So when you two leavin'?" Teddy asked.

"This weekend. Gene's taking us to the airport. Be gone ten days," I answered.

"Well, I hope you two have fun. Heather said Kelli ain't never seen a beach or the ocean," he said as he held his beer glass over his head, hoping for one more drop.

"Well, she hasn't since she was five or six," I said.

"You about ready?" he asked as he set the mug back onto the table.

"Thought you'd never ask. Let's ride to the dealer and check on the fellas," I responded.

He set a twenty dollar bill under his beer mug and placed it back on the table.

"Let's ride," I said.

"Glad you're back, Doc. It's damn nice havin' ya back," he said as he slapped my shoulder.

I remembered what he said, standing in just about the same place ten months ago.

You're a fucking doctor, for Christ's sake. And you're a doctor for the brain and all that shit. Knowing how a person's mind works. If anyone knows what people are thinking or ought to be thinking, it should be you. We all just want you back, Doc. We want you happy.

All Teddy wanted for me was to see me happy. Well, he was sure seeing that now. I've never spent a day happier in my life than I was spending them now.

"It's good to be back. Want to race to the Harley dealer?" I asked.

As soon as the word 'race' came out of my mouth, Teddy leaped over the handrail of the barrier fence, and took off in a dead run for his bike. Before I could step over the rail, his bike was started and he was pulling out of the lot.

Damn, he has lost weight.

Time passes and things change.

Chapter Twenty-Six

KELLI. Something about lying in the sun has always appealed to me. I love the feeling of my skin baking in the sun. Lying in the sun with Erik is so much better than doing it with anyone else.

Lying on the beach with Erik was better than I ever imagined anything could be. The only problem was that all he was wearing was a pair of shorts. Seeing him shirtless, shoeless, and wearing shorts was all I could take.

"Put on a shirt," I said as I looked at him putting oil on his legs.

"Yeah, right. This feels so good," he said as he exhaled and tossed the oil back in the bag with everything else.

"My beach my rules," I chuckled.

"Oh, believe me. I'm going to fuck you, alright. After seeing you all day in that bikini, you're going to get it," he said.

"I can't wait," I said over the top of my sunglasses.

I looked toward the ocean. It went on forever. As far as the eyes could see, there was nothing but ocean. Pictures didn't do a place like this justice. Erik said he would take me wherever I wanted to go, and I picked paradise. This had to be as beautiful of a place as God has ever created.

I watched as the waves eased in to the beach. It was hypnotic to watch. The same thing over and over, but in a different pattern. The thought of coming back to this place made me happy. Like our house, our coffee shop, and our Italian restaurant, this was *our beach*.

"I never would have guessed Bunny would have been able to build that addition on daddy's house like that," I said, turning to look at Erik.

"It looks really nice, doesn't it?" he asked.

"Yeah, but it's so funny. As soon as he got it done, daddy started talking about selling it and having Bunny build him a new, smaller house. Did he tell you that," I asked.

Erik turned to me and nodded. The thought of Daddy selling that house made me sad. I grew up in that house, and had many, many memories there. But now, I was older, I had a house of my own, and it was time for me to build my own memories in my own house. Daddy seemed to really like Bunny and that made it nice for both of them.

"Two more months," I said.

"Actually it's three and a half," Erik corrected me.

"No. Not for me. It's two. I don't count the month we're in, or the month of the wedding. Two more," I smiled.

"Girls and their counting," he laughed.

"What do you want to eat tonight?" he asked.

"Salad," I said.

"We've been here three days, and you've had salads every damned day," he said as he looked toward the beach.

"I want to keep my beach belly," I said as I patted my stomach.

"You don't have a belly, baby girl," he said as he stood up.

He walked over and kissed me lightly on the lips.

"You have a stomach, and a damned fine looking one at that. Let's go for a walk," he said as he reached for my hand.

I grasped his hand in mine and he pulled me from my seat. I grabbed our beach bag and put it over my shoulder. As Erik held my hand, we walked slowly toward the water. Walking with Erik along the beach was like a dream. When things like this happen, I try to make the memories last. It isn't very often a girl gets to live a dream.

As we walked along the beach, I kicked my toes in the water. I tried as hard as I could to remember coming to a similar beach when I was a kid with my father, but I had no real recollection of it. I doubt that I would ever forget this trip. Being with Erik was perfect, this beach was perfect, and seeing him barefoot and in shorts was even more perfect.

As we walked, I thought of meeting Erik and what had happened between us. I thought of the night I had to tell him about Columbia University, and how scared I was to tell him. I thought, even then, of how understanding he was.

The night that I scraped my knees up on the roof of the parking garage made me smile. Sucking his cock on the roof was so hot. I loved that. Erik was adventurous, but that wasn't all that he was. He liked to crawl inside my head and make me wonder things. He made me wonder about him, and he always made me wonder about myself.

Erik does all of the little things that I never really appreciated until one day when he explained them to me. He never has a long sexual encounter with me and just walks away. He always holds me and makes sure I settle down when it's over. He says it's necessary for me to come off of the emotional high of the sex.

He holds me and tells me that he is proud of me, and that I'm his baby girl. He massages my scalp, and rubs my shoulders. He tells me how proud he is of me and that I make him happy that I am able to do all of the things that he asks of me. Quite often, after sex, he asks me if everything was alright, and if I had any objections to what happened.

Erik wants what's best for me. Erik wants to make sure that I am as happy as he is.

I remember when he played the counting game with me at the Italian restaurant that day. I truly thought I was going to die. Simply die. I didn't know him very well then, and I wanted to impress him.

Kelli, I am going to count to twelve. Each time I count, I am going to slide my finger deep inside of you, and then pull it out. And when I slide it in, I am going to bang my knuckles against your little swollen clit. Do you hear me?

I think I squeaked.

I will take that as a yes. You will, Kelli, cum on the twelfth stroke, do you understand me?

He didn't know it, but I came right then. Right in my shorts. I knew on that day that I was never going to let him get away from me. I would be the most miserable stalker in the world if he tried to leave me after that day.

Twelve strokes, and he counted each one of them.

Thinking about it made me wet.

"Where'd you go baby girl?" he asked as we walked.

"What?" I asked.

"You were in a daze. I was talking to you," he said.

"Oh, I was thinking," I said.

"About?"

"That day at Il Vicino. The day we went to the mall after. The day you made me cum when you counted," I said as I looked his direction.

He chuckled and shook his head lightly.

"What?" I asked, looking up from watching the sand.

"That was priceless. I knew from the beginning I wanted you to be a certain person, because no matter who you were, I liked you. If you were the person I wanted you to be, sexually. Shit, I was screwed from the start," he said as he kicked at the waves.

"What do you mean?" I asked, watching my toes leave impressions in the sand.

"Well, I tried as hard as I could to get you to fuck up - to give me a reason to dump you. Hell, you never did. It didn't take me long to realize that you were the one for me. That day I burned my diary, I knew on *that* day I was eventually going to ask you to marry me. It wasn't long, and I was asking your father's permission," he said as he walked.

He stopped walking.

I walked until our arms were stretched, our hands barely grasping each other. I let go of his hand and turned around, facing him.

"Kelli, do you know, really *know* what you have to do to make me happy? To truly, deep down inside, make me happier than I have ever been?" he asked.

I shook my head.

He opened his arms.

I walked to him and hugged him. He leaned backward and looked down at me. As I looked up, he responded.

"All you have to do is exist," he said, and he kissed my lips.

Exist. That's all.

"All I have to do is…"

"Be yourself. Just exist. That's all. It's all I'll ever want from you. Just be alive and be on my left," he said.

"Deal," I said as I hugged him tightly.

I let go and stepped back and admired him.

"Get on," he said as he turned around, his back facing me.

"What?" I asked.

"Like a chicken fight. A piggy back ride. Get on," he said.

I jumped on his back and wrapped my arms around his neck. I slipped my feet through the loops he made with his arms.

As he ran for the ocean screaming, I knew that Erik Ead was going to take care of everything else.

All I had to do was exist.

Chapter Twenty-Seven

KELLI. I didn't want our vacation to end. It was the last day for us here, and it was early evening time already. I dreaded this actually ever getting here. We were scheduled to leave at six in the morning.

"What are you going to eat," he asked as he looked at the menu.

"I'm not really hungry," I responded.

"Baby girl, it had to end sooner or later. We'll come back," he promised.

I nodded.

"I know, I just...well, I just. I didn't want this day to get here," I said.

"Aww, baby. I'm sorry. Like I said, we'll come back. If you want, we'll come back every year. You look great after ten days in the sun, by the way," he said from across the table.

I felt sick.

I didn't want to ruin our last night at the beach, but I didn't feel like I wanted to do this. I didn't want this day to come, and I hated it that it was here. This was harder than I imagined it would be.

"How about something new. How about a salad?" he laughed.

I opened the menu and looked at it. Everything listed sounded gross. I couldn't even think about eating.

"Okay," I agreed, "Order me a salad."

"Okay," he said.

The waiter walked up to our table and smiled.

"Have we decided?" he asked, alternating glances between Erik and I.

"The lady will have the mixed greens salad, dressing on the side, add a grilled chicken breast to the salad, not on the side. I'll have the filet, 12 ounce," he said.

"Sides?" the waiter asked.

"Salad and green beans," he said.

I cringed.

The waiter nodded and walked away.

"Why the face, baby girl?" he asked.

"Green beans. Yuck," I said.

"Green beans are good," he said.

I shook my head and laughed.

"Nope, not anymore," I said.

"Why?" he laughed, shaking his head, looking surprised.

"This book I read. I'll never eat one again," I said.

"You need to quit reading that smut, baby," he laughed.

I nodded slowly.

Erik made me so happy. Even today, on a very tough day, he made me happy, and he made me smile. He orders my food for me. It makes me feel so good when he does it. I feel taken care of. I feel like he is in charge, and I feel like he actually does what he says, he owns me.

I like being owned.

By Erik.

I felt a little better as I ate the chicken off the top of my salad. Any food away from home always tastes better than the food you can get at home. Food in special places is always special. Always.

"This steak is marvelous," Erik said as he took a bite of his filet.

"You want to try it baby?" he asked.

"No thank you," I said.

"Green bean?" he asked as he picked one up from his plate with his fingers.

"Oh, God no," I said as he opened his mouth and sucked into his mouth.

He laughed.

He looked so good, wearing a light v-neck tee shirt, shorts, and sandals. I liked Erik the Dom, Erik the biker, and Erik the fighter. Something, however, about seeing him in shorts, sandals, and a thin t-shirt made him real. It made him seem so normal.

Not that he was abnormal. Heck, I would change nothing about him if I had a chance. But seeing him like this was just new, different, and satisfying. Yet another facet of the intriguing Mr. Ead.

As he finished his steak, I pressed my plate to the center of the table.

"Well, you look like you did pretty good," he said as he inspected my plate.

Baby Girl III

I smiled and nodded.

"Well, what do you want to do our last night here?" he asked.

"Well, let's pay for the meal and talk about it," I said.

"Well, what are you thinking?" he asked.

I looked at the table and then up at Erik

"I have a surprise," I said.

"Oh you do, do you?" he asked.

I nodded slowly.

"Well, tell me what we need to do," he said.

"Well, I need you to trust me," I said as I looked at the table again.

"Kelli, if you want me to trust you, you should look at me," he laughed.

He looked at the bill, and reached into this pocket for some money.

I looked up and into his eyes.

"I want to take you somewhere, show you something," I said.

"Okay, tell me where to go, we'll take the rental and go," he said as he started to stand up from his chair.

I shook my head.

"What baby girl?" he asked as he put his hands on my shoulder.

I pointed to his chair.

He squinted at me and walked back to his chair.

"What is it?" he asked.

"I need you to do something for me, and I don't think you're going to like it. It's important though," I said.

"Okay, what is it?" he asked.

"I need to drive. I want to take you somewhere," I said.

"Baby, it makes me nervous to have you drive. You've never been here, correct?" he asked.

I shook my head, "Nope."

"You don't know where anything is, correct?" he asked.

"Nope," I responded.

"Have you ever been where it is you're going to take me?" he asked.

"Nope," I responded.

"Why can't I drive?" he asked.

"Well, that's the thing. You're going to be blindfolded," I said.

"Excuse me?" he asked in a very harsh tone.

"Blindfolded. Erik, please, it's important to me. I need to show you something," I begged.

"You want to blindfold me in a place you've never been, to drive a place you don't know where it is, and show me something you've heard about, but have never seen?" he asked.

I nodded my head, "Please?"

SCOTT

He shook his head.

"I love you," he said as he shook his head lightly and looked up at the ceiling.

"I love you back," I said.

"Okay, let's do it," he said.

Chapter Twenty-Eight

*E*RIK. I listened as the navigation system made reference to the route. I tried, quite unsuccessfully, to determine where she was going. Not having ever been here before either, it made it difficult. Being in a place foreign to us, and going somewhere we've never been made me nervous.

I trusted Kelli, and the blindfold on my face was certainly proof of that trust. The entire trip, she didn't speak much. At first she talked, but she asked me to be quiet the last few times I had tried to talk. I decided to use this time in the car to relax and absorb some of the beach weather as it eased its way into the car window.

The smell of the beach was enough for me to know that we were still close to the ocean.

"Are we almost there?" I asked.

Silence.

"Kelli, if you're nodding your head, I can't see you," I laughed.

"Oh, sorry, I was," she laughed.

"Be quiet, I'm driving," she giggled.

I leaned back into the seat, grateful to have Kelli and her father in my life. I now have what I have yearned for. A family. A parental figure and a spouse. I felt as if my life were complete as she drove slowly through the neighborhood.

I felt the car slow to a stop. Kelli turned off the ignition. I heard her door open and close.

"Wait here for a minute, I'll be right back," she said.

I shook my head.

"No peeking," she said.

I nodded, "Yes ma'am."

She was gone for what seemed like an eternity. I heard footsteps close to the car.

"Kelli?" I asked.

The door opened.

"Come on, I'm going to take your arm," she said.

She led me by the arm for a considerably long walk. Finally, she stopped, and let go of my arm. I felt her hands behind me, and she pressed on my shoulders.

"Turn please," she asked as she pressed on my right shoulder.

I rotated to the left.

"Stop," she said.

I could hear her breathing behind me. I felt her hands on my head, untying the blindfold. As the blindfold fell from my eyes, I blinked at what I saw and where I was.

It was all too surreal.

Chapter Twenty-Nine

*E*RIK. As men, we are expected to stand tall. We are expected to always be able to protect those that we cherish. To be the one that is willing to do any and everything that may be required to keep the ones that we love from harm.

I have always believed that I was far more able to do this than anyone on or of this earth. I was certainly someone that could protect Kelli from any and all things that may harm her.

Until now.

"Erik," she said.

I stared straight ahead.

"Meet my mother," she stood beside me and stared straight ahead.

I looked at the gravestone.

Margaret Parks. January 13, 1950 – May 8 1991.

She died when Kelli was one year old, and was buried in San Diego. I now know why Kelli chose this place.

Surprisingly, she wasn't crying. I turned slowly and looked at her face. For once in my life, I had no idea of what to say.

"When daddy was sick that day, the day you left me in his hospital bed, he told me. He said he didn't want to die and have me not know," she said.

I nodded.

"Baby, I'm so sorry," I said.

"I'm not. I'm sorry she's dead. But knowing that she actually died is far more comforting than thinking she abandoned me. Daddy said he brought her here because he was scared. He was scared for people to know what really happened," she said softly.

I waited for her to continue.

"She died of a heroin overdose. He said she used the stuff since the war, on and off. She died right after Christmas. He drove her here in the snow. He said it was really cold. He used a truck. He told my grandparents, and that was all," she put her hands on her thighs and leaned forward and looked at the grave stone.

"He said he did it to protect me. He didn't want me to be ashamed. He said he was ashamed about how she died. He found her in the bathroom. I guess he would be ashamed. He apologized. After he brought her here, he said he kind of wished he could change it," she sighed and sat down on the ground.

Slowly I sat down beside her and wrapped my left arm around her shoulders. She leaned into my bicep and laid her head on me.

"He said after a few years, he even told himself that she walked off. He said he told the story so many times that he started believing it himself," she plucked grass from the ground as she talked.

"It's weird, but it's kind of a relief to come here and see this. I didn't know how well I would take it. It kind of puts closure to things. I'm sorry if I've been emotional or distant for the last few months, but I've been thinking about this," she said as she tossed the handful of grass into the air.

"Can we come back sometime?" she asked as she started to stand.

"Any time you want, baby girl. And I mean that," I responded as I began to stand.

"You know your father did this because he loves you more than anything," I said, looking into her eyes.

She nodded, "I know."

"He loves you more than anyone on this earth," I said as I kissed her forehead.

"I grew up, always believing that nobody on this earth could or would ever love me as much as my father," she said, her face buried in my shirt.

"Until I met you," she looked up into my eyes.

My entire life, I have never quite believed in love. I believed our parents just took care of us, were required to love us because we were their children, and love was something that was manufactured, developed, or built. It could never just exist, or 'be'.

Love is developed, and it is never perfect. We, as people, are flawed. Therefore, love is flawed. Most people live their lives trying to find the perfect person to provide them what they believe to be the perfect love. In my opinion, people should find someone that provides them with affection, someone that makes them feel, then develop and maintain the perfect love. That is the closest thing to real love that could ever possibly exist.

I remembered telling Kelli these things one day in the coffee shop.

I looked down into her eyes.

"I read a book once - about love that was developed and *love that just is*," I paused.

"And when I read the part about *love that just is* I scoffed. I knew better. I knew that it was merely words written by some shallow man that wanted to say what he had to say. And then I met you. And I now, Kelli, know what it is that books are written about. I know what people write poems about, I know what it feels like to know, and I do mean *know* what it feels like to be certain that someone loves you unconditionally. *Love that just is*," I placed my hands on either side of her face.

"Kelli Parks, I love you. From deep down in the pit of my being, I love you, and there's not a damn thing I can do about it. Because, Kelli," I inhaled a short breath.

"It. Just. Is," I kissed her lips lightly and looked into her eyes.

"I love you back," she said as she grabbed my hand.

My best advice to all living people is to keep searching. That person is out there. If you have to think about it, or second guess what you do have, it isn't love. Keep looking. Keep searching - because that person does exist. All you have to do is find them. And when you do, you'll know. You'll have what Kelli and I do.

Love that just is.

Made in the USA
Columbia, SC
27 November 2018